THE DIRTY DOLLAR

THE DIRTY DOLLAR

Gerald Hammond

Severn House Large Print
London & New York

This first large print edition published in Great Britain 2003 by
SEVERN HOUSE LARGE PRINT BOOKS LTD of
9-15, High Street, Sutton, Surrey, SM1 1DF.
First world regular print edition published 2002 by
Severn House Publishers, London and New York.
This first large print edition published in the USA 2003 by
SEVERN HOUSE PUBLISHERS INC., of
595 Madison Avenue, New York, NY 10022

British Library Cataloguing in Publication Data

Hammond, Gerald, 1926 -
   The dirty dollar. - Large print ed.
   1.   Petroleum industry and trade - Fiction
   2.   Suspense fiction
   3.   Large type books
   I.   Title
   823.9'14 [F]

   ISBN 0-7278-7203-6

Printed and bound in Great Britain by
MPG Books Ltd, Bodmin, Cornwall.

Prologue

She swam on, trying hard not to splash.

Mostly, she thought about surviving, about struggling on, trying to keep her head above water until she reached somewhere where she could pull herself on to land of a sort, but such primal thinking could not occupy the whole of her cerebral mind. Disorganized thoughts came and went, unverbalized and fleeting.

The Everglades. River of Grass, the Seminoles had called it. A shallow river, fifty miles wide. There were channels. There were islands. There were areas of reed that could be mistaken for islands. What was she swimming towards? Some of the grass was sawgrass which could cut you to the bone. There were alligators, creatures of eight or nine hundred pounds with a brain the size of a fingertip. And there were crocodiles. She had been told that they were not aggressive to humans except during the breeding season. This was the breeding season.

5

There were poisonous snakes.

There were areas of water lilies where you could tangle and drown.

How had a girl from an Aberdeenshire farm come to be swimming for her life, in Florida of all places? That phone call and what followed. A sequence of crazy, lucky breaks. She had thought it a lifeline, like winning the Lottery or the football pools. A death warrant.

It had begun before that, but how was it going to end? With a whimper and a splash? Was she just a chemical coincidence, to come and go without leaving any imprint on the world, food for some crocodilian? Did she not matter a damn in the scheme of things? Would she live on only as a tiny chemical signal in the memories of her parents and one or two friends, soon to be lost altogether?

She swam on, trying not to think about the alligators.

One

'Never,' said her father, 'never ever, start a sentence with "But you said".'

'But you *did* say,' Gillian Allbright insisted. 'You said, "Get a degree and you'll be sure of a job." You said that if I followed you into the farm I'd end up marrying a farmer and losing my figure and wearing myself out carrying bags of tatties around and having babies. That's what you said. Well, I did waste years of my life getting a degree and I can't get a job and I'm fed up.' She put her tongue out at him, half joking.

'I didn't say to get a degree in engineering,' her father pointed out. 'Employers are suspicious about how a young girl would fit into heavy industry.'

'I haven't got fat,' her mother put in complacently. 'And I've never carried a bag of tatties. Not a full sack. Just a carrier bag.'

'I don't need that sort of help,' the farmer said. 'The place is too small for that. And I'm only the tenant, so it isn't as though I could leave you the farm when I pop my clogs.' The three were lingering around the farmhouse kitchen after their evening meal. It had begun as a contemplative family discussion but it was becoming fractious.

'You have been offered jobs, Jill,' said her mother.

Jill snorted inelegantly. 'One job, in a huge drawing office as a junior draughts-person. A pencil-holder putting down other people's designs, and no prospect of promotion. I'd go mad in a fortnight. I want to use my education, meet challenges, find out if I have any skills. I want to be able to look back on something I've done as me. You understand? You, Dad, you have the satisfaction of seeing the land in good heart and your beasts healthy. Mum...'

'Yes? What am I supposed to be proud of?' Mrs Allbright asked comfortably. She was a placid woman, as plump as her husband was thin, rather as Jill imagined Jack Sprat and his wife.

'Given half a chance,' Jill said, 'you could be proud of *me*. But I'm not being given a chance and I'm too well qualified for other kinds of job. In commerce, they don't want people with degrees.'

'The real trouble is that you're too pretty,' Mrs Allbright said.

Gillian rarely thought about her looks, although the face which looked back at her in the mornings was properly symmetrical and deviated very little from the norm. All in all, she thought, it was a good sort of face and she was in no doubts about her figure. Her hair was fairish and the wave was natural, so she never had to bother very much about it. The unkempt look was high fashion at the moment. She might possibly have accepted being called beautiful, but pretty, never. 'Perhaps I should have thought about modelling?' she snapped. 'Or become a Page Three girl? I'd sooner become an honest tart – I'll bet there's more than a few student loans get paid off that way.'

'Now you're just being daft,' said her mother.

'Daft, am I? What I am going to do,' Jill said firmly, 'is stick a pin in the paper and wherever the pin sticks in I'm going to apply for the job. And if I don't get it, Dad, you've got a farm labourer and tractor driver whether you want one or not.'

Her mother occupied herself with pouring more tea. Jill was sometimes given to these extravagant statements and she usually meant them, but opposition would only harden her resolve. She had always been headstrong. Perhaps thrawn was the better word. Or stubborn. As a child, once she had made up her mind there would be no tantrums but no shifting her. Usually, although her desire might not be so acceptable to the rest of the family, there was sound sense somewhere in the background. Her mother recalled how Jill had taught herself to ride a bicycle by sheer guts and determination, angrily refusing all help, at the expense of the loss of much skin. Mr Allbright, on the other hand, remembered with little pleasure the time when Jill had wanted to learn the trumpet. She had got her way in the end. The house had become almost uninhabitable and the television relegated to late-night viewing. Jill had become competent on the instrument and had then virtually abandoned it, her desire apparently satisfied.

Jill's nostrils were flaring, a bad sign. 'Right!' she said. She reached out for the *Evening Express* from the sideboard, opened it at the Situations Vacant. She looked around vaguely for a pin. Her father had a box with two or three nails in his pocket, ready for odd jobs about the farm. Grinning, he took one out and handed it over.

Her bluff called, Jill closed her eyes, made several passes over the paper and lowered the point. She leaned forward to study the result. 'It's with Oltech,' she said. 'The big oil combine. Well, at least I'll have something to show for my work and I'll be on the spot when something more suitable opens up.'

'You sound as if you're sure you'll get it,' her mother said.

'I should get it, all right. It's for a cleaner.'

Despite her mother's horror and her father's even more irritating amusement, she did apply for the job and she got it, despite the reservations of the cleaning supervisor who decided to overlook Jill's decided overqualification on the ground that she was unlikely to miss shifts because of children's ailments, a husband on remand or what one cleaner had referred to as a hystericalrectumy.

In the following spring, to the amazement of everyone including herself, she was still in post. The job suited her remarkably well. Oil company business often continues in the evening and so the work had to be done through the night; but as long as it was accomplished thoroughly and during the hours while the building was otherwise idle, she was more or less free to vary her hours. Night work did not suit everybody, so it was remarkably well paid. She could fit in a social life in the evening, when she wished, although she had never been much for the gregarious life and she had no current boyfriend. She had resurrected her slight musical talent and occasionally stood in as guest trumpeter with a local band. A hand-me-down of what had been the family car, until hard use around the farm had virtually destroyed it, conveyed her to and from work at hours when the usual Aberdeen log-jams of commuter traffic were absent. There was some satisfaction in leaving the modern offices clean and fresh-smelling behind her and, while doing the work, she could wear her Walkman and listen to the music of the world, or catch up from cassettes with her study of business management with the Open University.

It was soon noticed that she was intelligent as well as efficient. She left every surface clean and every room aired and fresh. She never unplugged or switched off a computer which had been left on, nor discarded a piece of paper even if she found it on the floor; and while she might straighten the individual groups of papers on a desk, she would not have dreamed of muddling them together. She was soon promoted. The suite of offices pertaining to the most senior staff became her responsibility. She was even trusted to replenish the beverage machines and leave the money under lock and key for the head cashier.

After an initial period, during which she had to overcome the instinctive distrust of the educated by others, she got on well with her fellow cleaners. It was customary to take a tea-break at around one in the morning, and to foregather around the coffee machine on the sixth floor although most of them brought flasks and sandwiches. On these occasions, there would be jokes about the happenings within the company and gossip about the affairs of the staff, but often Jill listened with respect to tales of the Good Old Days.

The whole building had been built for Shennilco but, after a major scandal and some financial reverses, Shennilco had been taken over by Oltech. The American giant had immediately transferred all major management decision-making to Head Office in Miami, slimmed down the Aberdeen staff and let the lower half of the building to associated oil-related firms. The best of the old staff, faced with reduced responsibilities and an almost certain lack of promotion opportunities, had trickled away and the upper ranks of what remained were, in Jessie's words, 'a bunch of deadbeats'. The cleaners took a keen interest in the fortunes of their employer, always reading the company newsletter and clipping out of the *Press and Journal* any items of news which the others might have missed. Jill thought that their combined knowledge of the company's business probably exceeded that of the average member of the executive staff.

★ ★ ★

One night in April, a clear night showing false promise that spring might after all be about to arrive, proved a turning-point in Jill's life.

She might easily not have heard the telephone. She was busily hoovering the carpet in the General Manager's room. Her Walkman was playing one of her favourite tapes of instrumental jazz and she was singing softly, improvising wordless melodies, harmonizing a descant to the big band of Buddy Rich. But as she worked round to the far side of the big desk, the flex caught under a corner. She switched off the vacuum cleaner while she sorted out the tangle and at the same moment *Chicago* came to an end. She lifted one of the earphones to listen.

The telephone was not only sounding its electronic note but it was managing to do so in a manner which conveyed both impatience at having been neglected for so long and an absolute determination to continue ringing until either Doomsday arrived or somebody answered it, whichever came first.

Jill's first impulse was to lift and replace the receiver, thus cutting off the annoying interruption and teaching the telephone a lesson in good manners. But, although the phone has only been in common use for a mere four generations or so, Jill admitted to herself that the compulsion to answer a ringing phone is already imprinted in our genes. (When she came to think about it, she found this strange because, surely, those who could resist the siren call of the telephone would have more free leisure for procreation. She was given to such fruitless speculation when her mind was not fully engaged elsewhere.) She selected the correct phone from the two on the desk, lifted the handset and put it to her ear. 'Oltech,' she said briskly, just as she had often heard on the lips of late-working staff.

'Mr Hochmeinster is calling Mr Fiddich,' said an equally brisk female voice with a pronounced American accent. 'Put Mr Fiddich on the line, please.'

Jill was aware that Mr Hochmeinster was the President, the Chairman, the Founder, the Panjandrum and absolute boss of Oltech (US) Inc. His bulldog features, unflattered by the photographer, glared from the top left-hand corner of the front page of each company newsletter. She knew that he was regarded with awe and discussed in whispers. She suspected that sacrifices, possibly human, were performed in his honour. And she could hardly not know that Mr Fiddich was the General Manager of

Oltech (UK) Ltd, because his nameplate had stared at her every night from the desk. She put aside her Walkman. 'Mr Fiddich is not in the building,' she said.

'To whom am I speaking?' the American voice enquired loftily.

'My name is Allbright,' Jill said.

'You are an executive?'

'Not exactly. I am an employee.' Jill kept amusement out of her voice.

'Who else is available?'

'There is nobody else in the building,' Jill said, 'except the cleaners.' The word *other* somehow became submerged. 'After all, it is after midnight here.'

'Hold the line, please. I am putting you on hold.' The earpiece began to play Vivaldi's *Four Seasons*, one of the few pieces of music which Jill actually disliked. She settled, smiling, into Mr Fiddich's luxurious executive desk chair. A few words with the Almighty would make an entertaining break in a dull shift.

The voice came back on the line. 'Mr Hochmeinster wishes to know the present whereabouts of Mr Fiddich.'

The General Manager's diary was open on the desk before her. 'Mr Fiddich is in London at the Oil By-products Conference,' she reported.

'Do you have a telephone number for

him?'

'I'm afraid not.'

'Hold the line, please. I am putting you on hold.'

Jill was developing a dislike of Mr Hochmeinster's secretary, or whoever the other might be. Nobody with an American accent, she felt, had any right to use such perfect, pedantic English. 'If you do,' she said, 'I shall hang up.'

She waited. It wasn't much of a job anyway.

'I *beg* your pardon?' said the voice. People, it seemed, and especially fellow and subordinate employees, just did not say that. After a further delay she repeated, 'Hold the line, please.' There was the sound of a receiver being laid down and receding footsteps, all the way from Miami, but no Vivaldi. Jill grinned to herself. She had enough of being pushed around in her childhood and at school and university. Nobody, but nobody, was going to push her around over the phone from a great range.

The footsteps returned. 'I am putting you through to Mr Hochmeinster,' said the voice. *Now you'll catch it,* said its tone.

'Hello there,' said another voice. It did not sound like Mr Hochmeinster's photograph, being deep and rich and sounding slightly amused. In his photograph, which showed

17

him as bald and with dewlaps, the bulldog looked ready to bite somebody in the leg. Staff sometimes worked very late and Jill had heard many accents during her time with Oltech; this one, she thought, was Texan, but with a resonance all its own. 'Hochmeinster here. What's this about you not being put on hold?'

'For one thing,' Jill said bravely, 'I have my own work to do. For another, I hate Vivaldi.'

'I go along with you on both counts,' Mr Hochmeinster said. 'Can you give me the home phone number of any of the senior staff?'

A quick glance at Mr Fiddich's desktop and upper drawers produced nothing more useful than a staff telephone list, and since that consisted of no more than a string of names and extension numbers it was of no immediate help. 'Not immediately, no,' Jill said. 'I'm sorry.'

'Listen, I don't know who you are, but if you're the only staff working you'll have to help out. The shit's hit the fan. You know about the pipeline through Scotland?'

From the newsletters, Jill was aware that the company was responsible for the laying of another pipeline to carry natural gas between Aberdeenshire and the north of England, on behalf of a consortium of users. 'I know of it,' she said.

18

'We have a whole shipload of pipes due to arrive in Aberdeen round about now. That's a whole lot of pipes. You know that the company depot in Aberdeen's out on strike?'

'First I've heard of it,' Jill said. Having gone so far, she was going to have to tell somebody about it. She took a sheet of paper out of Mr Fiddich's drawer, picked up one of his pencils and began to make notes in her tidy hand.

'First anybody's heard of it. The depot manager's on holiday. They seem to've timed it for maximum effect and for just after all the offices shut down. News only reached me an hour ago. What they're asking for's twenty-five per cent increase in pay, a month's paid vacation, increased pensions and hospital insurance. And these are just workforce. If they get it, the rigs and platforms will be after the same. It's out of the question and they know it – they're just out to do damage.

'So the pipes can't go to the yard. I've spoken to the harbour and they can't give us space – they're already stacked up and there are two container ships due. And our ship has to be unloaded come whatever – have you any idea what demurrage costs? That's what you pay when you delay a ship from getting on with its next cargoes.'

From his tone, she gathered that demurrage would be expensive. 'A lot,' she said respectfully.

'A lot is right. One hell of a lot. Abercorn Transport – the haulage contractor – is waiting for fresh orders and there'll be somebody in their office all night. Well, we can't do it all from this end, not in a couple of hours. I've got to get home – some damn dinner my wife's set up. I'll leave it in your hands. Get hold of whoever you can, sort something out and there'll be a bonus coming your way. They can settle the strike on more reasonable terms, or maybe the ship can divert to another port if that'll minimize the delay. Maybe offload the pipes on to some of our rigs, though I doubt if they could accommodate more than a fraction without coming to a halt. Tell them to do something. There are times in life, young lady, when nothing's the best thing to do; but this is not one of them, not when there's a ship to unload and the ship has other cargoes waiting. I'll phone you in a couple of hours.'

'Mr Hochmeinster,' Jill said, 'you don't know who I am.'

'Miss Allbright, I don't care who you are, you're all there is. It's in your hands.'

The line went silent.

★ ★ ★

Oltech had saved the top six floors of the Shennilco building for its UK executives and the higher those staff climbed in the hierarchy the higher also their offices rose. The General Manager's room, with its understated luxury inherited from a preceding Chief Executive, was on the twelfth floor, at the very top of the building. Jill sat back for a moment and looked unseeing over the lights of Aberdeen. Earlier, those lights would have glittered like a carpet of jewels all the way to the seafront, but now they were reduced largely to street lamps and the lights of vehicles travelling on errands mundane or romantic. Out at sea, she could see the navigation lights of a large vessel approaching the harbour – quite probably the ship bringing Oltech's pipes.

Jill's first impulse was to decide that Oltech's problems were not hers. But she was an employee of the company and, having already overstepped the mark, she had to do something. She had been well paid for most of a year.

Another scan of Mr Fiddich's desk did not produce a staff home telephone list, miraculously appeared since the last time that she looked, but there was a telephone directory for north-east Scotland in a bottom drawer. Only three Fiddichs and the initial, according to his nameplate, was C. Jill knew how to use the PABX – the cleaners sometimes had to call home during their shifts and as long as the traffic was kept within reasonable bounds the firm turned a blind eye to the practice. She dialled 9 for an outside line followed by C. Fiddich's number. At the other end, a phone rang and rang before a sleepy female voice answered.

'Mrs Fiddich? I'm speaking from the Oltech office. There's an emergency. I need to contact your husband urgently.'

'He's in London,' said the voice through a yawn.

'I know he's in London,' Jill said. She tried to keep impatience out of her voice. 'Do you have a number where he could be reached?'

'His secretary would know.'

'Do you have a number for his secretary?'

'No, I don't.'

Jill took a still firmer grip of her patience. 'How can I reach him?' she asked slowly and distinctly.

The voice made an audible effort to pull itself together. 'I have a number where the conference is being held, but he's probably staying at his favourite hotel. I have that number somewhere...'

'You phone him,' Jill said firmly. 'His job may be on the line and he's needed back here urgently. Get hold of him and tell him to phone the Oltech Aberdeen office, his own extension. Will you do that?'

'I'll try.'

Jill dashed out of the room, took the stairs at the south end of the building and skittered down two floors to the hallway and waiting area on the tenth floor, where the cleaners were already gathered for their tea-break on the seats in the waiting area between the lifts and the cashier's office. Mugs and packets of biscuits were set out on the two coffee-tables and a vacuum cleaner stood ready on the industrial-weight carpet to pick up any crumbs.

Jessie, who was responsible for the tenth floor and half of the eleventh, raised her eyebrows and a thermos flask, but Jill shook her head. 'No time for that,' she said. 'There's an emergency. Fay, your man works at the depot, doesn't he? Did you know that they're on strike?'

Fay, a formidable woman with a pronounced bust and very blonde hair, shook her head, but gently so as not to disturb the carefully fixed curls. 'I came away before the bugger was home,' she said. 'And he'd probably not have telled me anyway. He kens damn fine I don't hold with strikes and he's already been offered more money at Smith and Murieston only he'd have to do some work there instead of idling around waiting for the next busy spell. I'll give him laldie when I see him.' It was Fay's unshakeable belief, common among the cleaners, that industrial action usually cost more in lost wages and the risk of lost employment and goodwill than it gained in benefits which would probably have arrived anyway in due course.

'There was a phone call to Mr Fiddich's room,' Jill explained rapidly. 'There's a ship coming in with a huge load of pipes and the transport's standing by and now there's nowhere to put them. It's going to cost the earth if it isn't sorted out and they have to delay unloading the ship. Mr Fiddich's in London. Does anybody know how to reach any of the other staff?' There was a general shaking of heads.

'Mr Gordon's the Personnel Director,' Maggie said. 'He'd know.'

'What's his first name? Or initial?'

'No idea.'

There would be columns of Gordons in the phone directory. Gordon is the premier local name.

'Who's the top dog in engineering?'

'That's Mr McRobb. But he's out on one of the rigs,' Jessie said. 'He stayed late last night, waiting for the time for his flight, and we had a wee blether. He's a friendly old lad but he told me hissel that he was getting past it.'

'And logistics?' Jill asked.

'Mr Brown,' said Maggie.

'Maggie,' Jill said, 'Personnel's among your offices, isn't it? Help me out. Nip along and see if you can find Mr Gordon's initial or his home phone number or, even better, a list of staff home numbers. I was offered a bonus if we can sort this out, so we'll share it around if we get it. Will you help?'

Despite the cleaners' motherly contempt for the senior Aberdeen staff they had a loyalty to the company whose fortunes they had followed, in some cases, for years. The mention of a bonus gave their loyalty an extra stir.

'I'll try,' Maggie said, She was a thickset woman with greying hair and a determined expression. 'But Mr Gordon locks his desk and files every night. Very partic'lar about it, he is.'

'Give it a go anyway,' Jill said. She was beginning to buzz. 'Fay, will you phone your man? See what you can find out about this strike.'

'I'll do that. If the bugger's hame.'

With the departure of Fay and Maggie, Jill was alone with Jessie and a small woman from one of the offices below. 'This is our problem, Hester,' Jill said. Hester, reluctantly, left.

'Jessie,' Jill said, 'I'm just thinking aloud.

25

Even if we can get hold of staff, they'll need somewhere to put the pipes and it all takes time which they haven't got. This time, time really is money. A whole shipload of pipes. That's going to take a whole lot of space ... ground ... land. Maybe we can prepare the ground for them.' She snapped her fingers. 'Ground again. Ground's the problem. What does that make you think of?'

Jessie was an older woman than the others with a pert and wrinkled face and gnarled hands. Her face lit up in a grin, chasing the wrinkles into new patterns. 'The farms?' she said.

'Exactly. Your husband farms somewhere to the south, Portlethen way, doesn't he?'

'Aye. But it's no more than a smallholding, mind.'

'No matter. He'll know the larger farmers round about. And my dad farms north-east of here. You phone your husband and I'll phone my dad and we'll get them asking around the farmers for who has a bit of ground to spare, not for very long – it should all be away before the harvest, so the vacant ground where they store their straw bales should be available. It would have to be level and somewhere that a big vehicle can get to. Tell them ... say that, if it comes off, they'll be paid.'

'How much?'

Jill swallowed nervously. It was all moving a bit too fast. 'If it's necessary – if, mind – say a thousand each, give or take, depending on how big the area is. Would that get them moving? The money's gone out of farming just now.'

'No bother.'

'Remind him to find out roughly how much ground each farmer can spare and how to get there with an articulated lorry.'

Jessie's lips were moving with the effort of memorizing her instructions but Jill knew that she could carry them out to the letter.

Jill retreated upstairs to Mr Fiddich's room again, settled in the soft leather chair and phoned her father. Mr Allbright was none too pleased at being woken in the middle of the night, and out of a rather pleasant dream if he could only recall it. He dozed through a dozen rings in the hope that the caller would give up or that his wife would rouse and answer it; but the extension had been installed on his side of the bed, against his outspoken wishes, so he rolled over and lifted the receiver. He jumped at first to the conclusion that Jill had suffered a breakdown and he began a lecture on the subject of how he had told her from the start that she would have to budget for breakdowns and that she would have to subscribe to a breakdown service;

27

but when Jill managed to break in, he was pacified by the gift of a perfect excuse to wake up some of his more prosperous rivals who he suspected of looking down on him for the modesty of his acreage. The chance to earn some extra money did not come amiss either. His daughter, fingers crossed, held out the hope of a small additional bonus for each additional farmer he could recruit. He came fully awake. 'They can use my land between the barn and the burn,' he said. 'It doesn't grow worth a damn anyway.' He was already reaching for his warm dressing-gown.

With the call finished, Jill leaned back in the chair. Her business management course had made it clear that the first rule of good management was to find the right people for the job, brief them properly and leave them to get on with it. She looked at her watch. The night was trickling away and she still had her own work to do. She jumped up. Luckily, she had finished with the vacuum cleaner. With the doors propped open, she should be able to hear the phone even from the toilets. She refilled the soap dispensers and toilet-roll holders and then set to with mop and bucket.

The sound of the telephone fetched her through to Mr Fiddich's office. Somehow the bleeping sounded plaintive and lacked the urgency of command of the earlier call.

'Oltech.' She had adopted the singsong tone that she had heard on the lips of the other staff.

The voice, this time, was one which she had heard on rare occasions when its owner had worked late. Its tone was even more querulous than usual. 'Who's that in my room? And what's this about?'

The first question was too reminiscent of 'Goldilocks and the Three Bears', so Jill ignored it. 'Mr Fiddich, did you know that there's a strike at the depot?'

'I had some word of it, yes. There's not much I can do about it from here.'

Jill had an immediate mental picture of the balding, middle aged but ancient-looking man hurrying out of harm's way and hoping that his staff would solve his problems for him. 'This is Miss Allbright,' she said. No need to mention that she was only a cleaner just yet. It was rumoured that Mr Fiddich, who was not the most dynamic of managers, was only acquainted with the topmost echelon of his staff. 'There has been a call from Mr Hochmeinster. A ship carrying pipes for the pipeline is due in and there's nowhere to put them. Can you give me the home phone numbers of the staff who should deal with it?'

'I don't carry phone numbers in my head.

Ask Jim Gordon, the Personnel Director.'

Jim. That might help. 'I will if I can reach him,' Jill said briskly. By now, she had the bit firmly between her teeth. Her parents would have recognized the signs. Once Jill saw an objective she would go for it and not even a granite wall would stop her. 'In the meantime, I'm making enquiries of the farmers, to see who could allocate some ground to store the pipes. If I don't hear anything to the contrary, I'll tell Abercorn Transport where to take the pipes. Do you agree?'

'Oh, yes. Yes, I suppose so.' He was, Jill decided, a straw blowing with the wind.

Jill looked at her watch again. 'I shall be speaking to Mr Hochmeinster soon. May I say that I have your authority to proceed on these lines?'

'Of course, of course.' Jill had the impression that Mr Fiddich would have agreed with almost equal enthusiasm to having his nose-hairs plucked. 'Tell him that I shall be coming back on the first morning flight, to take over.'

'Very well. Goodbye.'

Jill was beginning to enjoy herself. Nothing is quite as much fun as chasing other people around. She looked up Abercorn Transport, keyed the number and picked up her pencil. A voice acknowledged that it was indeed Abercorn Transport. While she waited for the call to be answered, she flipped through the telephone directory. There was a column of J. Gordons in the directory, most of them within commuting distance of Aberdeen.

A voice on the line interrupted her. She jerked her mind back. 'Oltech here,' she said. 'Who do I speak to about the pipe shipment?'

'Mr Gates is waiting for your call.'

Mr Gates came on the line. 'Thank the Lord,' he said. 'The ship's just coming in but I'm told that your depot's strike-bound. Not having heard from you, I was just about to stand the drivers down.'

'Don't do that. Go ahead and load up. I'm fixing up storage space on farms.' She was struck by a thought. 'There won't be cranes. Can you manage to unload?'

'That won't be a problem. I can send machinery where it's needed. You'll pay for the hire?'

'Of course,' Jill said loftily.

'And there will be extra mileage.'

'Give me some figures so that I can get them authorized.'

Five minutes later, she was finishing in the toilets when Maggie appeared. 'I can't find those numbers.'

Jill leaned on her mop. The pressures of executive command could get a little wear-

31

ing. 'Then ... the PABX is in your area, isn't it? See if there are any staff home numbers there. Failing that, call every J. Gordon in the book, Aberdeen first and then working outwards.'

'Oh my!'

She was stowing away the tools of her trade in the cleaners' cupboard when Fay came panting up the stairs. 'Wait while I tell you!'

Jill saw no need to talk on the landing while they could be comfortable and handy to the phone. She led Fay into Mr Fiddich's office, showed her graciously to the visitor's chair and settled again into the executive swivel where she was beginning to feel at home. 'Tell me what you've found out.'

'Well now.' Fay settled herself comfortably and adjusted her bosom. 'My man says it's all because the depot manager, Mr Syme, is away in South Africa on his holidays, visiting with his sister. Dougie Falls, who's also the shop steward, was left in charge – the system usually runs itself – but he went off on a sick line. Something was dropped on his foot. His deputy as shop steward is yon man Herb Spicer and he's a rough-spoken commie bastard, my man says. He's been waiting a chance to get back at the company, ever since he was passed over for supervisor – passed over because of a lack of

32

loyalty, Jim says. There's irony for you!

'So Herb called a meeting and said it was time they had better pay and conditions and they could catch the company with its breeks down. The men wasn't for it, mostly. They're already getting better money than most.'

'Then why did the idiots go along with it?' Jill asked.

Fay bridled. 'I'm just *telling* you. There's some rough buggers among the men and yon Spicer has them in his pocket. He doles out ... substances.'

'Drugs?'

'Not the real bad stuff, heroin and the like of that. Dougie Falls would never have stood for it. But amphies and pot, he's the man to go to. Some of the men are what you might call dependent on him and they're not the brighter or the better ones. My man says that those ones were backing Spicer and the others were waiting for a lead and they didn't get it so they just went along. I told him he was a spineless wallydrag and he needn't think he'll get his drinks and smokes off my wages while he's out.'

Jill jotted down the names but decided not to commit the allegations to paper. 'Well done,' she said. 'And, Fay, would you do the Board Room for me? I'd better stay near the phone.'

Fay rose, groaning, to her feet and said that she was pleased to help. They were both remembering an occasion when Fay had been rather under the weather after an evening out with her husband and Jill had laid her out in the VIP suite and shared her work with the others.

Maggie appeared in the doorway. 'I found Mr Gordon's number,' she said. 'In his out-basket, there was a bittie of his home note-paper with a heading. I called him. He didn't like it one bit but he's coming in.'

Two

For a few blessed moments there was peace. The silence seemed almost overpowering. Jill managed to drink a few sips from a mug of tea out of her thermos and look out of the window. The first glow of dawn was beginning to show over the North Sea and the first signs of the morning rush hour were beginning to show in the street below. She could have leaned back and fallen deeply asleep. But soon the first names of farmers willing – or eager – to give space to pipe storage began to come in and she was busy relaying them to Abercorn Transport and recording them in her notes. It was all moving at an increasing pace. She began to feel that she had a tiger by the tail. She was walking the precarious tightrope between self-doubt and overconfidence, but walking it without toppling off.

Mr Gordon, the Personnel Director, came bustling in. He proved to be a harassed, balding man, hastily dressed and unshaven but retaining his self-importance. His greying hair was grown slightly long, parted in the middle and slicked down – a style which struck Jill as distinctly Edwardian. Jill had not met him before – he considered the engagement of cleaners to be beneath his dignity and he left it to their supervisor. Jill was momentarily relieved that she had removed her overall and that, having been to the cinema with a friend, she was wearing a modestly respectable frock instead of her usual jeans and T-shirt.

His eventual arrival promised Jill a respite but at first his presence was simply one more distraction. He arrived while Jill, with a road atlas open on Mr Fiddich's desk, was trying to convey directions for reaching a farm which she knew so well that she had never had to take note of road numbers or signposting. The lorry driver being hard of hearing and still driving his vehicle throughout the discussion made communication even more fraught. It seemed that Maggie had left Mr Gordon with no very clear idea as to the nature of the emergency and he jumped at first to the conclusion that she was on a personal call. It was only by dint of grim determination, a raised voice and a refusal to acknowledge his presence that she managed to complete her explanation and disconnect, with a silent prayer that the

instructions had been received and understood.

Between concern that a coach and horses
were being driven through all proper
procedures and indignation at having been
hauled out of his house without adequate
sleep, a proper breakfast or time to shave,
Mr Gordon was more than a little agitated.
He attempted to tower over the seated Jill,
though a certain lack of stature robbed the
attempt of its effectiveness.

'Just what the hell is going on?' he demanded. 'Why have I been called in before
dawn? What's the emergency? And who the
hell are you? One of the cleaners? What are
you doing, sitting in Mr Fiddich's chair and
using his phone ... and...?'

'If you'll let me speak for a moment, I'll
try to answer the first six of your questions,'
Jill said severely. Jill had no intention of
standing up. Having already overstepped all
reasonable bounds, she saw little reason to
grovel now. She decided to keep her temper
and behave with dignity. 'There was a phone
call from Mr Hochmeinster—'

'You have no business, answering the
phone, ever!'

'It rang on and on and I only picked it up
to say that there was nobody in the building
but the cleaners. And you should be very
glad that I did answer it,' she added, remem-

bering, 'because what was going wrong was going to cost an awful lot of money and Mr Hochmeinster was not very happy about it. So, because I was the only person on the spot he could get hold of, he left it with me and he's going to call back.' She paused to draw breath. 'And I tried to get hold of any members of staff to take over but if there's any list of home numbers we couldn't find it, but Maggie got your number somehow.'

Mr Gordon began to calm down. 'You still haven't told me what the emergency is,' he pointed out.

Jill began a careful explanation of what she had been able to find out and the action so far taken. 'I found Mr Fiddich's home phone number in the directory and I called his wife and she called him and he phoned here. He agrees with the action I've taken. And now I'll be quite happy to dump the whole thing in your lap, if that's what you want,' she said. (Mr Gordon paled and appeared to shrink even smaller.) 'But I suggest that you get on the phone to the right members of staff and get them to come in and take over.'

Mr Gordon was nodding. 'Perhaps Malcolm McRobb...'

'He's offshore,' Jill said.

'So he is. His depute, then. And Ed Brown. I'll phone from my office.'

The phone began to demand attention again.

Jill treated Mr Gordon to a faint smile. 'And are you telling me not to answer this?' she enquired.

Mr Gordon looked properly disconcerted. 'I suppose you'd better carry on, now that you've started,' he said. He scurried out of the room.

Jill dealt with a call from a lorry driver who had become hopelessly lost among the small roads between Maryculter and Stonehaven and another from a farmer who wanted to know why he had not been included when remunerative extras were being handed out.

Mr Gordon returned, bringing with him the air of one who had single-handedly resolved the whole crisis. His appearance had improved and she realized that he was now neatly shaved. He must have kept an electric shaver in his desk. 'Edward Brown and George Wallis are coming in,' he reported. 'George is Malcolm McRobb's depute.'

Jill was tempted to keep him standing in front of the desk, but he seemed to have accepted her as a colleague and almost as a natural leader, so she conveyed by body language an invitation to him to sit down. She nodded. 'Tell me something,' she said. 'Did you know about this strike?'

Mr Gordon paused in the act of lowering himself into the chair and then completed the movement. 'Well, yes.' He recalled who he was addressing and inflated again. 'But that's none of your business. How dare you ask me that?'

'Mr Hochmeinster will certainly want to know,' Jill said. She was sorely tempted to tell him that he could go now, but she had pushed it as far as it would go and the phone was demanding attention again.

This time the voice had the deep tone and Texan accent of Mr Hochmeinster and it held the warmth of a man who had wined and dined well. Jill imagined that she could hear him puffing on a large cigar. Not Havana, of course, because Cuba was a dirty word. 'That damn dinner was like to go on for ever,' he said, 'or I'd have called an hour back. How've you got on? I've felt like I was sitting on an ants' nest all evening.'

'Two staff are on their way in,' she said. 'Mr Fiddich will be on the first shuttle back in the morning. Mr Gordon's with me now. Meanwhile, I've fixed with a lot of farmers that the pipes can be unloaded on ground that won't be needed for a couple of months. I'm afraid we'll have to pay them. That plus the extra transportation are going to cost.'

'How much?'

Jill had already added an estimate of the extra haulage cost to a guess at the number of farmers requiring payment. She scaled it up to allow for contingencies and again to translate it into dollars. 'About forty thousand dollars,' she said, 'but some of that will come back because there won't be so far to haul the pipes from the farms to the pipeline.' It sounded an awful lot of money when she said it aloud. She waited for the storm to break.

'Peanuts!' said Mr Hochmeinster. 'Demurrage would have cost at least ten times that, more like twenty, depending on how long we delayed the ship. If it all pans out, you'll get your bonus.'

Jill had been remembering some of the facts given in the company newsletter. 'Work on digging for the pipeline starts next week,' she said. 'I thought of suggesting that the last few loads go straight to the site.'

'That's a good thought. Stay with it.'

'And I've found out a bit more about the strike. The depot manager's on holiday, the shop steward's off work with an injury and his depute as shop steward has a chip on his shoulder. You know the expression?' she asked anxiously.

'I know it.'

'Apparently he has some of the tougher men in his pocket because he dishes out dope to them, and they intimidated the others.' She hesitated. 'None of this is really my job, but I think I'd be going way over the top if I was to...'

'To call the cops? You're right again,' said Mr Hoch meinster. 'That's not your job, it's a personnel matter. Put Jim Gordon on the line when we've finished. You've done well, young lady. You *are* young?'

'You may think so.'

'I did think so, from your voice. Tell me a little about yourself.'

There didn't seem to be a lot to say. 'I'm a farmer's daughter from Aberdeenshire. I have an engineering degree and I'm just finishing a course in business and management.'

'Has Jim Gordon seen your certificates?'

'No, not yet.' She kept her voice firm and steady. 'Mr Hochmeinster, I think I should explain that I'm only working as a cleaner.' She hurried on. 'Because I'm a girl, I can't get a proper job in engineering so I've been working as an overnight cleaner while I chase other qualifications which might help me to land a proper job.'

His laugh came booming over the wire. 'Hell, I guessed it was something like that. Who else among that bunch of layabouts would be working after midnight? Your voice sounded intelligent, you couldn't have made

42

anything much worse and I've always reckoned that a minnow on the spot was worth more than a big fish on the other side of an ocean. And I was right, wasn't I? I wasn't hoping for more than that you'd get some of the staff out of their beds and back on the job, but you've gone a lot further and not put a foot wrong, far as I can tell. Show Jim your certificates and if they check out I'll maybe have something better for you. Put him on now.'

Jill handed the phone across the desk. She gathered up her notes. In a mood of sudden exhilaration, she had the illusion that she was walking three inches clear of the carpet as she went through into Mr Fiddich's secretary's office, much more functional and less luxurious than his, to copy her notes on the photocopier. The machine differed from the one which she had used at university and it took her a little time to get its measure, but she called it a rude name and it quickly learned obedience.

When she had finished, Mr Gordon was standing in the doorway. 'Mr Hochmeinster says that you're not a cleaner any more.' Mr Gordon sounded dazed but relieved to be back on familiar ground. 'You report to me when you've been home and had some sleep. First, he wants you to stay and brief Ed Brown and George Wallace.'

Jill was ready to drop. 'Couldn't you do that?'

'Not on your life! And Mr Hochmeinster wants you to find out who knew about this strike.' The words seemed to be dragged out of him on a rusty chain. Jill decided that Mr Gordon felt vulnerable. She felt rather vulnerable herself. Carrying out an inquisition of strange senior staff was asking a lot of a raw girl. But before she could protest, the phone was at work again. Mr Gordon waited in silence while she received and passed on to Abercorn Transport the names and locations of what, on the basis of very rough calculations by Abercorn, she hoped would be the last of the farms.

Messrs Wallis and Brown arrived almost together. George Wallis, the Depute Engineering Director, was little more than Jill's own age, tousle-headed and unshaven (although it needed a close look to detect his sandy stubble). His voice was definitely public school though possibly Scottish – Glenalmond or Gordonstoun. He was not ill-looking, although Jill sensed that he might rather fancy himself. His looks were marred rather than enhanced by an exaggerated Cupid's bow of a mouth. He had thrown on the first clothes to come to hand, but his shoes were brightly polished. Ed Brown, the Logistics Director, on the other hand, had paused to shave and had brushed what little hair he had. His tie was off-centre but otherwise he was almost dapper except for his dusty shoes. Sherlock Holmes, Jill thought, might have deduced much about their characters or their womenfolk from those shoes, but for the moment she remained unenlightened.

Mr Gordon, by way of introduction, did no more than state names. He went on to say, 'Mr Hochmeinster decided to leave matters in Miss Allbright's hands.' He had, with difficulty, recovered a little of his dignity and his tone was meant to convey that he considered Mr Hochmeinster's decision to be whimsical.

After going so far, Jill had no intention of being patronized. She seated herself firmly in Mr Fiddich's chair and motioned the others into the humbler chairs beyond the big desk. Better get the bad news over first, so she assumed her stiffest manner. 'I only came into this because I happened to be in here as a cleaner,' she said, 'but Mr Hochmeinster himself spoke to me and because nobody else was available he asked me to do what I could about a shipload of pipes and a strike at the depot. I spoke to Mr Fiddich in London but I had great difficulty reaching any other staff, so I have taken certain actions of which, I may say, both Mr

Fiddich and Mr Hochmeinster approve.' She handed over copies of her notes and spent several minutes in further explanation of her night's work.

'You seem to have done your best,' Mr Brown said coldly.

He was not going to get away with damning with faint praise. 'What would you have done in my shoes?' she asked.

While the Logistics Director hesitated, George Wallis was more generous, or more conciliatory. 'If she hadn't done her best, our heads would have been on the block,' he pointed out. 'And a bloody good best it was. We couldn't have done better.'

'Thank you,' Jill said. 'It's your baby now, but I suggest that you arrange for the last loads of pipes to go direct to where the first pipes will be needed, wherever that may be. And I'll leave you to sort out the precise costs of these arrangements. I'll come back to the office later today, in case you want to know more precisely what was said to each farmer and to Abercorn.' She paused. She suspected that their heads might well be on or close to the block but she decided to break the news as gently as she could. 'Finally – and this wasn't my idea – Mr Hochmeinster directs me to get an explanation of how this strike managed to occur without anybody doing anything

46

about the consequences. No, not now,' she said quickly when all three men tried to speak at once. 'I've been up all night and I'm going home to bed. I shall come in again later today. Good day to you.'

She left them to sort it out between them and walked out. Her friends, the cleaners, had already dispersed to their homes. In her car, lit by the brightness of the dawn, she pulled into a layby and unwound like a suddenly released spring. It had been her first taste of power, almost her first real challenge, and she had won through. And, by great good luck, she had been *seen* to win through. A huge bubble of relief and joy was expanding inside her. If Mr Hochmeinster was as good as his word, she might have an inside track to a proper job. She pounded the steering wheel and shrieked with manic laughter until a milkman stopped his float and came to see if she was all right.

Three

Jill had never needed more than a few hours of deep sleep, which was one reason why the overnight cleaner's job had suited her. Following her extraordinary night of challenge and adventure, she woke in time to prepare and eat a substantial brunch, choosing from her inadequate wardrobe the dress that she considered most nearly suitable for office wear. Neither of her parents was around, but the front of the old stone farmhouse with its drape of ivy seemed to be smiling at her. She left an uninformative note.

She was in a mood of joy, confusion and disbelief. She drove into Aberdeen through a dull, damp spring day, but she only saw that the leaves were out on the birch trees, rock plants and daffodils flourished in the gardens and on the farms the earth was tinted green. She went over the night's events in her mind and realized that the sun was not, after all, shining. Her mood began its descent. She asked herself if those events could really have happened. Had she been hallucinating? Would she arrive at the Shennilco building to find that nobody had ever heard of her? Or had the whole affair been a dream or a monstrous practical joke? Would the staff be lined up to laugh at her? Worse, would there be cameras, hidden or not?

The early afternoon traffic was comparatively light and she slipped quickly through the silver granite streets and was there before she had quite nerved herself. She had never before seen so many cars in the staff car park, which was large, shaded in summer by its pattern of mature trees and embellished with flower beds raised by stone walls. She found a slot and walked to the main doors on rubber legs and with a hollow feeling in her chest.

At night, only a side door had been in use. In contrast, the main entrance hall by day looked vast and almost crowded. She was expected. The well-groomed lady behind the desk addressed her by name after no more than a moment's hesitation, handed her a pass already made out in her name and told her that Mr Gordon was expecting her, meanwhile regarding her with friendly curiosity as one might look at a strange but cuddly animal. If tales of her night's adventures were already circulating, they must

49

really have happened.

Jill took the lift to the ninth floor and found Mr Gordon's office. The door was open and the Personnel Director was already looking out for her. The receptionist, Jill decided, must have made quick use of the internal telephone. She had known the room well over the previous months but it looked quite different with the incumbent in occupation. Mr Gordon was much more friendly, even respectful, in manner. He glanced at Jill's slender collection of certificates and made a few notes, but absent-mindedly.

'Faxes have been flying to and fro,' he said. 'We're directed to find you an office.'

'To myself?' The height of Jill's ambition had visualized her only as relegated to the corner of a large drawing-office.

'Certainly to yourself. The only room vacant is the one that Mr Fiddich had when he was depute to the former Chief Executive. We were going to do some shuffling around but Mr Hochmeinster said that that room would be very suitable, so that's where you're going; and what we'll do if Mr Fiddich ever gets the depute he's been arguing for, God alone knows. I'll have your degree and certificate put on your desk. You know the room?'

'I've dusted it every night for almost a

50

year,' Jill pointed out.

Mr Gordon's expression suggested that he would have had more tact than to remind Miss Allbright of her humble beginnings. 'I was going to phone you at home if you hadn't arrived very soon,' he said. 'Mr Hochmeinster will be arriving on the shuttle and he wants you to go out to Dyce and meet him. Nobody else, just you. You have a car?'

'Only an old banger.'

Mr Gordon looked shocked at the very idea. 'That would never do. The company doesn't run its own pool cars – we found that they might stand idle for a month and then we'd need half a dozen simultaneously. We use taxis and a hire-car firm and of course staff use their own.' He leaned back and tapped a coded signal on the partition behind him. 'Miss Law will phone for a car. You're to wait near the luggage carousel at the airport. Mr Hochmeinster has been given a description of you.'

'I'd know him anyway, from the photograph on the newsletters.'

'Not *the* Mr Hochmeinster,' Mr Gordon said. 'He never leaves the Miami office. This is Mr Hochmeinster Junior. His son. Mr Benjamin. He does his father's running around for him, acts as trouble-shooter and so on. I've never met him myself, but I'm told that he's what they call a tough cookie. He certainly carries a lot of clout. Perhaps you would give him this?' He handed over an envelope and then looked at his watch. 'You have nearly an hour. I'll take you up to your room.'

'I know where it is,' Jill said. 'And perhaps I should see Mr Fiddich?'

'You probably will, if he's in. He came in this morning, checked on what was going on and I think he went out again.'

It all seemed too easy. Jill had had much the same sensation when she picked up a box which should have been full and found it to be empty. 'Shouldn't somebody be telling me my job description? I don't know what to call myself or what my salary is or anything.'

For the first time, Mr Gordon became quite human. He raised his hands in a gesture of helplessness and pulled a face. 'My dear,' he said, 'I'd tell you all about it if I could. That's my job. But I just don't know. Frankly, I don't know what the ... the dickens is going on and it's all irregular and unprecedented. Head Office is dealing with it at the moment. I don't even know if you're to be attached to the Aberdeen staff or employed from Miami. My guess is that they're waiting for a report and recommendations from Mr Benjamin. There are some papers on your desk and they may help. Come back to me if you have any problems and I'll help if I possibly can.' *But don't expect miracles*, his tone suggested.

He went so far as to rise from his chair as she left the room – which, to Jill, was the strongest reassurance yet of her new status.

On the twelfth floor, the office which had been empty for as long as Jill had worked for Oltech now showed signs of imminent occupancy. While not as big as Mr Fiddich's room, it seemed imposingly large and nearly as well furnished, with almost as deep a carpet. It seemed that the levels in the hierarchy were scrupulously reflected in the furnishings. She sat and looked around. Her office. *Her* office. Charcoal carpet, off-white walls, oatmeal upholstery and, on the walls, colour pictures of oil rigs, platforms and tankers. She had seen all these things before, but now they had the fresh significance of being hers. When she came to look in the desk drawers she found a selection of all the usual pencils, notepads and staplers; but on top of the desk she found that the 'some papers' referred to by the Personnel Director comprised in fact several neat stacks of files and folders.

The more she looked at the papers the higher the mountains seemed to grow. From a week's solid reading it began to look as though she had enough material to keep her at work for a lifetime. Could she make a career out of reading papers? One lecturer on the Open University course had warned aspiring managers to watch out for that very inactivity. She was wondering where to begin when there came a tap at the door which connected with the secretary's cubby-hole. A woman, little older than herself, stood in the opening. She had a cloud of naturally red hair and a pert face which broke easily into a smile. 'Miss Allbright? I'm Sheila Dobson,' she said. 'I'm Mr Fiddich's secretary but I'm to do your typing for you until you get an assistant of your own.'

Jill was relieved to meet a truly friendly face. She got up and shook the other girl's hand. 'You'll have to steer me through the pitfalls,' she said.

'From what they're saying, you don't need much steering. Is it true that you answered the phone to the Mighty Monster last night and sorted out where all the pipes were to be stored?'

'More or less. I'll be happier when I've sorted out where all these papers are to go.'

'I bet,' Sheila said. She examined the stacks and made some adjustments. 'These on the left are all basic information about the company and how it works. The booklet on top is the company bible to read, mark, learn and inwardly digest. Frankly, if you learn that by heart you'll be pretty well shatterproof around here. The others you could take in your own time. The middle lot are for information about ongoing work; just read the last couple of entries in each, initial the slip and stick the file in your out-basket.' With an effort, she picked up the third pile. 'This lot are the minutes of past meetings. I'll put them into your filing cabinet and help you find what you want when you need to. Do you feel better now?'

'Much better,' Jill agreed.

She settled down to investigate the company bible while Sheila stowed away the minutes and withdrew to her own cubicle next door. The chair was a slightly smaller version of Mr Fiddich's. Evidently someone's nicely tuned judgement of the gradations of rank extended to the hierarchy of backsides.

The company bible was complex but it presented a clear picture of the mechanisms by which the organization functioned. She was busily digesting the first sections and slotting them mentally into her Open University course material when one of the two phones on her desk buzzed discreetly. Her car, a voice told her, was at the door.

She collected more curious glances on her

way through the entrance hall. Outside the main entrance she found not the humble taxi which she had expected but a vehicle which, although not stretched, undoubtedly qualified for the description of limousine. Jill thought that she knew her way around Aberdeen, but the uniformed driver wafted her effortlessly by roads which bypassed the more serious bottlenecks, sometimes on streets which she recognized but often along byways which never quite turned out to be dead ends. Suddenly they were at the airport roundabout on the main Inverness road. At the airport, he parked squarely outside the main doors and took up his stand beside the car in a manner which dared anyone to try to move him on. Either he was well known there or there was a dispensation for limousines, because nobody tried.

The monitors indicated that the shuttle was on time, but she had a few minutes to browse the bookshop. Then she took up her station beside the carousel. Passengers began to trickle through. After another delay, luggage appeared on the carousel.

The man appeared suddenly in front of her, already carrying a small bag. Her first impression was that he was big, but well proportioned and certainly not fat. There was some of his father's bulldog look in his square face but on him it was softened into something which was only just on the tough side of good-looking. He had removed his soft hat and his black hair was only slightly ruffled. How he had managed to come off a long flight and a shorter one and still arrive cleanly shaved and with his palely striped shirt looking fresh from the laundry she could not guess. His suit, obviously expensive, was unwrinkled and his shoes were brightly polished, but where Ed Brown, the Logistics Director, would have looked dapper he only looked well presented. He carried with him an air of ... what? Power? Wealth? Confidence? At least two out of the three, she decided.

If Jill was impressed, Mr Hochmeinster Junior seemed less so. As a cleaner, Jill had seen little need to improve on the student's informality of dress. She was suddenly very conscious of her mother's second-best handbag and a dress which was a leftover from her student days, but she managed to shake his offered hand and ask him how his flights had been.

'Endless,' he said, moving towards the entrance doors. 'Concorde used to be much quicker. I suppose the French could be trusted to litter their runways and ruin things for everybody else.' Jill seemed to recall that the plane which had dropped the lethal litter on the runway had been

American, but she held her peace. His voice was less aggressively Texan or else the telephone had exaggerated his father's drawl.

At the pavement, Mr Hochmeinster headed automatically for the limousine and stood aside for Jill to enter first. He said a few words to the driver. The driver held the door for them, which was more than he had done for Jill alone. When they were moving, he seemed to be in no hurry and she soon noticed that they were taking a more roundabout route than before.

'Mr Gordon asked me to give you this,' Jill said.

He opened the unsealed envelope, scanned the single sheet quickly and glanced up to be sure that the glass partition was closed. 'Quick work,' he said. 'What did you think?'

'I haven't seen it,' she said. 'It was addressed to you.'

He made no comment. She was left to wonder whether it had been some sort of a test of her discretion. Instead, he said, 'My father was very impressed by you.'

'But you're not,' she remarked. 'Mr Hochmeinster, please remember that I was only a cleaner twenty-four hours ago.'

His expression still showed no reaction although if she had been looking at him full-face she might have detected a glint of amusement in his eyes. 'Miss Allbright,' he said, 'in the first place, I think you might call me Mr Benjamin. All the other staff do, to distinguish me from my father and from several cousins. In the second place, I am not forgetting that you were working as a cleaner. Nor am I forgetting that you have a degree in engineering. To an American, there is nothing unusual about a college graduate filling in by doing manual work – it is part of the culture. In the third place, in business at least, I never mean more or less than what I say. Hints are so often a waste of breath and, just as often, a clear message is imperative. I said that my father was impressed, and that is exactly what I meant. Any impression that I may have gained was at second hand, but clearly you had the guts to accept a challenge, the lateral thinking to perceive a solution and the resolution to put it through virtually single-handed. You did well.

'The note, if you had read it, would have told you that the haulage and stowing of the pipes is going like clockwork. It would also have told you that Spicer, the man behind the strike, has been arrested on a charge of possessing illegal substances with intent to supply. The police intend to hold him until tomorrow morning at least. The shop steward, Falls, is being brought in by wheelchair and a meeting with the strikers has been arranged for six p.m., local time, to-night. I mentioned to you that my father was impressed, only as a preamble to saying that he wants you to attend the meeting with me, as an observer and, if appropriate, to contribute. As you may have gathered, he's a great believer in letting local staff use their local knowledge.'

His grammar, she noticed, was, like his manners, perfect. Jill suspected that his might be the inspiration behind the secretary's too-perfect diction, but she knew that the upper levels of American education were very good. Was this the product of Yale or Harvard?

'I'm sorry,' she said. She left a short pause in case her apology should be taken as referring to her next words. 'But I don't suppose that I'll open my mouth. I've no experience of attending a meeting to resolve industrial disputes.'

'Right. Your degree is in engineering. Mechanical?'

'Yes.'

'Good. We don't have to run the meeting – that will be the shop steward's job. But watch and absorb. Dad wants you to gain experience in management. You already defused this strike. You also produced the information which removed the man Spicer

60

from the equation. We'd like the strike settled but – and don't quote me on this – we're saving money while it lasts because, once those pipes were in store, the depot would have been quiet for several weeks. So, if the men insist on making the company a present of their wages for a period, it would seem ungracious to refuse.' Jill glanced quickly at his face but was unable to read it. 'We were going to offer five per cent at the next negotiation and that's as far as we'll go. I'll make that clear. Beyond that point, you'll be free to have your say.'

'And I'll be judged on it?'

This time he really did produce a smile of sorts. 'Perhaps, If you do pipe up, I think that you'll do all right, but I'll be on hand to jump in if I'm needed. My father's a great believer in throwing people in off the deep end. And so am I.'

'So it's a test?'

'See it that way if you like. We have good reason to assess your strengths and probe for weaknesses. I'll explain a little further.' He glanced again at the glass screen. 'I told the driver to take his time so that we could talk in absolute confidence and what I'm about to say is very definitely not for repetition.'

'You can trust me,' Jill said.

'I believe I can. Very well, then. The

61

company's North Sea operation has been troubled and less profitable than it should be. Part, but only part, of the reason may be that Mr Fiddich looked good as Depute General Manager, so he was moved up to fill the vacancy. Now it's becoming clear that he was riding on the back of his old boss. Frankly, the British operation is failing. Given a weak man at the top, he's not going to promote anybody stronger or better qualified than himself. The weakness spreads.'

Jill had read *Parkinson's Law*. 'Injelitance,' she said. He looked puzzled. 'A mixture of incompetence and jealousy,' she explained.

'Right. Ideally, we fire the whole lot; but we need continuity and we can't tell, from a distance, which heads should roll. Dad's first thought was to put you in as Fiddich's depute.'

The very idea scared Jill almost out of her wits. 'Good God, no!' she said.

'No,' he agreed. 'It would never have worked. Fiddich would have had control over you. What Dad wants is somebody with local knowledge and some knowledge of engineering, and with no personal loyalty to the existing staff, reporting directly to him. If you make the grade, he wants you to be his personal assistant, his eyes and ears in the Aberdeen office.'

The prospect was almost equally daunting but it began to make a sort of sense. 'And your task is to vet me for that job?' she asked.

'That's what he suggested that I do, although I rather think that he's made up his mind. In the first instance, we only want unbiased reporting of staff strengths and weaknesses and especially loyalty, to confirm what we're already sensing from long range. But there's one more aspect to your task.' He paused and turned his head to make eye contact. 'This is just as confidential as the rest or even more so. Two phone calls have reached Head Office, each hinting that some member or members of staff were ripping off the company. Each came from a former member of staff and might have been written off as the malice of a disaffected former employee, except that the calls came from two different and unconnected men, neither of whom had any cause for resentment; and the British end does seem to show above-average costings. The auditors, James and French, were highly recommended to us, but you may be able to look into their standing. You can't duplicate their job, but you can keep your eyes and ears open and report anything of significance. There may be hostile forces at work. We have suspected a whispering campaign and there have been one or two minor incidents which may have been sabotage. Yes?'

'I suppose so,' Jill said faintly. 'I can watch and listen and if I hear anything, or if it stares me in the face, I'll report it.'

'But be discreet. It may be coincidence, but one of the two men who made the phone calls was injured when a piece of drilling equipment fell on him. The other now refuses to speak to us.'

Benjamin Hochmeinster's manner, being both polite and serious, had led Jill at first to regard him an unbending older man – a tough cookie, in Mr Gordon's words, very cold and distant. But he turned towards her and produced again a trace of a smile, faint as starshine on a dark night but enough to soften his bulldog features. Now that her first trepidation was wearing off, she realized that he was not so very old, perhaps seven or eight years older than herself, and was capable of seeming comparatively human. A good education and too much responsibility at an early age, she decided, must have forced on him a maturity and discipline that made him seem older and harder.

'We don't expect miracles,' he said. 'I'll explain a little further. We see the audited accounts and all the reports and minutes, but they only tell us what somebody wants us to know. An intelligent person on the spot – and you are both of those – has more chance of seeing or hearing or smelling something that doesn't seem quite in keeping with the rest of the pattern.

'Add to that the value of local knowledge and contacts. The stranger doesn't know who to speak to, nor what value to place on inflections in the local dialect. Even body language varies from place to place. Again, you have the advantage of being a woman.'

Jill was amused. 'You believe in female intution? Or do you expect me to use feminine wiles to coax the information out of men?'

He took her question quite seriously. 'Nothing like that. Women have superior communication skills. That's all that female intuition really is. So give us your opinions of the other staff. Give us your thoughts, your gut feelings, your intuitions if you like. Given a starting point, we can do the rest.'

Jill was feeling her way through a maze of barely seen factors. 'Wouldn't it make more sense just to put in a new General Manager?'

'You're quite right. But Charles Fiddich will retire next year. Meantime, the man we trust and want to take over is doing a contract in Malaysia and can't be spared. More

65

to the point, if he goes in cold they'll close ranks on him. Somebody local with a dispassionate overview might give him a chance to make the right choices as to who goes and who stays.

'One other thing. You may think me paranoid, but I want to stress that you should keep that side of the work confidential. Write nothing down. Leave nothing on your PC.'

'I don't have a PC,' Jill said.

He glanced at her once, clearly feeling that anyone lacking such an amenity must have had a deprived childhood. 'You know how to use one?'

'We used them all the time in college. I just couldn't afford one of my own.'

'You'll be issued with one. Store your information on floppy disks and keep them with you. We'll also fix you up with some special software so the files are shredded on the PC and no one can recover the information. Speak to my father or to me, person to person. I'll authorize Supplies to fix you up with a cellphone – much more difficult to monitor – and I'll leave both numbers with you. My number is available, day or night. Don't hesitate, if you need advice urgently or have news to pass on.

'And now, we must prepare you for the meeting. You won't carry any weight if you look like a student,' he said. (Jill gave him full marks for guessing the provenance of her dress. Mr Benjamin had been around women.) 'You need something a little higher up the market.'

Jill's father had owned a substantial farm until a combination of setbacks followed by the liquidation of a major firm of grain merchants had forced him into liquidation. Her parents, Jill knew, had made sacrifices to help with her education. Even so, she was still struggling to pay off her student loan. That she had been a mere cleaner twenty-four hours earlier was no secret. If Mr Benjamin thought less of her for being broke, well, damn him! 'I don't have any money,' she said.

He seemed neither surprised by the statement nor impressed by her frankness. 'Of course not,' he said gently. 'But I'm to authorize the bonus that my father promised you. It should cover your immediate expenditure, unless you have it in mind to buy a yacht or an executive jet.' (Jill looked at him sharply. In the sudden swirl of events, she could almost have believed that he was not joking, but his impassive face had softened slightly. She smiled and shook her head in reply.) 'You will be drawing a salary which I think you will find adequate and, of course, any expenses incurred on the company's business will be reimbursed. In case of any further difficulty, a float can be arranged. For the moment, we can use the firm's credit card.'

Jill could see other problems arising. 'I promised a share of the bonus to three of my fellow cleaners,' she said. 'They helped me out by making phone calls and ... and things. If you like, I called on them for their local knowledge.'

He nodded approvingly. 'But the moving spirit was yours. If your colleagues went beyond their normal duties, I'll see that they each get an appropriate bonus. Would a hundred pounds each seem adequate?'

'I expect so.'

'Your bonus is yours,' he said firmly.

'Thank you. But nobody had told me yet what salary I'm to get.'

'A fax will be on the way from Miami. I could make a guess.' He mentioned a figure which, even after she had knocked off a third to convert it from dollars to pounds, took her breath away. 'I'm talking pounds,' he added. 'You seem surprised. But you are not a cleaner any more. Salaries soon get noised abroad. Oil company executives are well paid and they won't respect you if you're working for a secretary's wage. Only monkeys accept peanuts.

'And now, we had better get on with

preparing you for the meeting.' He tapped on the glass screen and the driver slid it open. 'Take us to a good shop for women,' he said. 'What's your mobile number?'

The driver recited a number from memory and the screen closed. Mr Benjamin produced a telephone from his pocket. It was slim and lightweight but, when he opened it, Jill thought that it had every communications facility known to modern man and could probably have guided the space shuttle to a safe landing. He keyed the number into its memory and slipped it away again.

Four

Jill was feeling stunned by the sudden rush of obligations. She decided to push them to the back of her mind, for digestion later and alone. She was wondering what on earth to say, when Mr Benjamin saved her the trouble. 'Are you hungry?' he asked.

'Not very.' The upheaval of events and imminent challenges had scared her appetite away.

'I don't seem to have eaten seriously for days. Shall I drop you at a good shop and pick you up later?'

Jill braced herself for more admissions. 'I'm not as much of an idiot as I must sound,' she said, 'and I'm not usually too bad at clothes, but I've no experience of business. I want to get it right but I've no idea what would strike the right note. Could you bear your hunger for a little longer and come in with me?'

He looked at his thin gold wristwatch. There was no maker's name on the face, which alone suggested to Jill that it was hugely valuable. 'We have time for both,' he said agreeably. Jill decided that he was too good to live. In her, admittedly limited, experience the average man would rather stand naked under a cold shower than accompany a woman into a shop.

The car set them down in Union Street. Mr Benjamin said a few words to the driver and the car slid away through the traffic. Inside the shop, they were met by a dignified saleslady. 'You want a business suit,' he told Jill. 'With your colouring, I suggest black or navy. A simple blouse and suitable pantyhose.' He exchanged a glance with the saleslady.

Left to her own devices, Jill would have spent hours in indecision; but Mr Benjamin waited patiently and when she emerged from the fitting-room gave an immediate nod or shake of the head. In less time than she would have believed possible, her old clothes were in a carrier bag, he was settling what seemed an enormous bill by credit card and whisking her along the pavement to a shoe shop. Ten minutes later, she tidied her hair and was surprised to see in the shop's long mirror the very image of how she would have expected a yuppie business-woman to look. Without more than a glance of consultation, Mr Benjamin added a quality handbag. He keyed two digits and spoke into his phone.

While they waited for the car, Jill worried. Was she really expected to fork out this astronomic sum? Or were these gifts, in exchange for which she would be expected to sleep with him? She was not wholly inexperienced, though her two brief affairs with fellow students as inexperienced as herself had been physically unsatisfying. She looked at him doubtfully. He was very much a man of the world. Americans, she knew, could be very rude or amazingly polite, and his remarkably good manners would almost certainly continue between the sheets...

He intercepted her glance and she had an uncomfortable feeling that he interpreted it accurately. 'The account will come to you eventually,' he said. 'Discuss the payments with Charles Pringle, the Finance Director. I'll suggest the same basis as a car loan. But, since you're starting from scratch and we don't have to help you with removal expenses or rehousing, I think the company might pay half. Is that satisfactory?'

'Very,' she said. The word came out on a sigh of relief. 'Thank you.'

'Not at all.' The car oozed to a halt beside them and he ushered her inside. 'Caledonian Hotel,' he told the driver.

Jill was still half-expecting an invitation to his room but she found herself at a table in the almost empty dining room. She managed to swallow, and enjoy, a plate of ham and salad while her host put away a large steak and, emerging at last from his stiff business shell, chatted knowledgeably and amusingly about the trivia of the day. He ate neatly. He ordered a wine by name, but when it arrived she noticed that it was Californian. She accepted two glasses, to boost her confidence.

The depot turned out to be a group of low buildings of brick and slate, straggling around a large yard which was partly cluttered with alien machinery and materials, not far from the harbour. The squat figure of Mr Gordon, the Personnel Director, met them at the door of the offices. He beat the driver to it and held the limousine door respectfully. If he was surprised by Jill's presence and suddenly improved image, he hid it well.

Jill, as the newcomer, felt out of place in introducing two old colleagues to each other but Mr Gordon had told her that he had never met Mr Benjamin. She muttered an introduction.

Mr Benjamin put out his hand. 'Good evening,' he said. 'What's the situation?'

Mr Gordon shook the offered hand respectfully – Jill thought that for two pins or less he would have kissed Mr Benjamin's signet ring. 'They're waiting for you inside,' he said. 'Douglas Falls has already had a word with them. He let it be known that he doesn't approve of their actions, but as shop steward he has to go along with the vote already taken. Now they're waiting to hear the management's response. There's less than a dozen present.' He lowered his voice. 'There may have been some intimidation.'

In the world of business, Jill decided, when it came to genders, all were equal but some were more equal than others. The principle of ladies-first applied or not according to the circumstances and attitudes. Thus Jim Gordon led the way inside but Mr Benjamin gestured to her to precede him. So far, Jill had got by on the confidence of youth and the knowledge that she had little to lose; but now she was being, perhaps deliberately, manoeuvred into a position from which she could most disastrously fall on her face. She was expected to join in the debate. Or was it a test to see whether she had the sense to keep her mouth shut? The safest course would be to assume so. She found that her knees were uncertain and her mouth had gone dry.

She hung back for a moment. 'You'll help me out if I go off the rails?' she asked softly.

He smiled and nodded and immediately

74

she felt more secure. 'You won't,' he said. 'But I've already told you that I'll be in your corner.'

Comforted, she hurried to catch up with Mr Gordon.

The meeting was taking place in the canteen, a workaday room the size of two squash courts, painted institutional cream and green. Some of the small tables had been pushed back to make space, but two had been put together to make a sort of top table beside which a man who had to be Dougie Falls was established in his wheelchair. He was a large, square-jawed man with a well-tended head of silver-grey hair. He was incongruously dressed in a neat jacket, shirt and tie but with pyjama trousers above his shoe and sock. Presumably the plaster encasing his damaged foot would not pass through the leg of his daytime trousers.

Three of the men stood to one side as if distancing themselves. They were more roughly dressed and altogether scruffier than the rest but somehow managed to convey that they held themselves to be superior. Seven or eight others stood aimlessly in the open space, like sheep awaiting a leader. As the three representatives of the company took their seats, there was some audible muttering from the three separated men who she had no difficulty guessing to be the followers of Herb Spicer, the absent agitator.

Dougie Falls twisted round in his wheelchair to rap on the table with his knuckles. Silence fell. 'I'm here representing the union. We've already heard from the floor,' he said tersely. 'The terms of the last resolution have been put to management. Let's hear from Mr Benjamin.'

Benjamin Hochmeinster smiled. 'The demands made in that resolution would put you roughly on a par with offshore supervisors, divers and specialists and close behind departmental deputes. You must know that that's unrealistic. Every other person in the company would demand an equivalent raise and the cost simply could not be borne.'

'Right, that's it,' said one of the three of Spicer's adherents. He was a big man with red hair and a raucous voice. 'They're not going to listen to us. I move that we adjourn the meeting.'

Dougie Falls said, 'Those in favour?'

The three troublemakers and one of the others raised their hands. 'We second the motion,' they added in unison.

'Motion lost. Now let's be more realistic and hear what management will offer.'

'Thank you,' Mr Benjamin said. 'As far as

the North Sea operation is concerned, we're in a highly competitive field. Management has to consider the well-being of the whole company and the jobs of a great many employees—'

'You're just blethering,' broke in the man with red hair. 'Get to the point or let's be getting hame.'

'Very well, then,' Mr Benjamin said grimly. 'We're offering five per cent.'

Few of the others present seemed surprised, but the three made loud noises of amazement and disapproval.

'Hear me out,' Mr Benjamin said loudly. 'There's just so much money to share around and there are more than you to be paid out of it.'

'We've seen the figures,' called out the red-haired man. 'We saw the profit the company made last year. It was in the papers.'

'That was the company as a whole and included Alaska, the Gulf of Mexico and Malaysia, all more profitable than the North Sea.' Mr Benjamin paused.

'All that profit was after wages was paid,' said one of the red-haired man's companions. 'It went to the shareholders.'

'Fuck the shareholders,' said the red-haired man.

'That's stupid,' Jill said. She was startled to find that she'd spoken aloud.

'Stupid, is it?' demanded the red-haired man. 'Are we going to stay here and be called stupid by a wee lassie, no more'n a bairn?'

There was a silence. They were looking at her. Jill got to her feet, numb with stage-fright. She wondered whether bursting into tears might not get at least some of the men on to her side. Then a surge of anger took her by surprise. A stranger inside her spoke before she had time to think. 'Maybe. And any child could see that you're making a childish mistake here,' she said. There were small snorts of resentment. She ploughed on. A few words from her management course came into her mind. Her voice sounded squeaky. 'Do you – do we – have a pension scheme?'

'A damn good one,' Dougie Falls said. 'We fought for it and we got it.'

'Then you're shareholders,' Jill said. The silence changed its wavelength, from anger to shock. 'If not in this company then in others. Insurance companies and pension schemes have most of the money which would otherwise be lying idle. How would you feel if workers somewhere else, working for companies in which your pensions are invested...' she paused and drew a breath, because bad language had not been part of her upbringing – 'if they were to say, "Fuck the shareholders"? How many employers can you think of that went out of business because your friends said, "Fuck the shareholders"?' She braced herself for another effort. 'So before you say "Fuck the shareholders", just remember who you're preparing to fuck.'

She went on quickly before anyone could point to any gaps in her argument. 'When I said that you were making a mistake, I meant that you were showing the company that they don't need a depot at all. A depot costs the earth to run, probably more than it earns when you remember that its facilities may lie idle for months. The trend today is to dump surplus materials, hire or lease equipment—'

Jill hesitated for a moment. There had been a reaction in the room. Somewhere in the room had been a sudden exhalation, of amusement or something else, and she thought that one of Spicer's three cronies had frowned. She ploughed onward. 'To rent storage on a temporary basis when it's essential, have materials delivered on board or direct to sites and return machinery to the agents for servicing between contracts. Or, even better, to engage contractors to do the work.' She paused again and drew breath. 'What you did was to shut down the depot at what seemed to be a critical moment. You were looking to hurt the company. You cost the company some money, but a drop in the bucket compared to the expense of running the depot. In fact, you showed the company that it can manage very well without you.'

'That was your doing,' said the third of the troublemakers. 'Wee bitch.'

'If it hadn't been me, it would have been somebody else,' Jill said bravely. 'In return, you cost yourselves a lot of hours on time-and-a-half—'

'Double time,' said Dougie Falls.

'There you are, then. You're still losing wages and the company's doing well without you. You're in great danger of persuading the company that it doesn't need the depot. If you hold out for your demands you'll make sure of closure, because you know as well as I do that you've as much chance of being the next Scotland football team as of getting what Herb Spicer talked you into asking for. Mr Benjamin just offered you five per cent, and that isn't a negotiating figure, it's a last word, take it or leave it. That's all that I have to say.' She was tempted to add something ironic about *babes and sucklings* but the right sentence refused to form.

There was a silence. Jill wondered whether they were waiting for her to say more.

'On that note,' Benjamin Hochmeinster said, getting to his feet, 'I think we should withdraw and let the meeting consider Miss Allbright's words. Another meeting may be called for next week or the week after to hear the union's reply, which will be given due consideration.'

Jill, dazed, found herself outside. She was ready to enter the limousine again but Mr Benjamin made no sign. 'That went very well,' he said. 'Perhaps Mr Gordon would give you a lift back to your car on his way home?'

'Yes, of course,' said the Personnel Director.

Mr Benjamin offered Jill his hand. 'We shall be in touch,' he said and, ducking into the limousine, was borne away.

In Mr Gordon's nearly new Rover, Jill was conscious of anticlimax. 'Did I do all right?' she asked.

Mr Gordon chuckled. He looked ten years younger. 'Don't you know when you've carried all before you? You did very well. They won't want to lose wages for another week or more. In the morning, they'll come begging to settle. Mr Benjamin would have been shouted down if he'd said what you said, but you could get away with it. He was delighted.'

'He didn't say so.'

'He may have felt inhibited by my presence. Top management sometimes likes to bestow its accolades in private.'

Jill was still ready to search for flies in the ointment. 'You live in Cults, don't you? Dropping me back at the office car park would have been nearer for him than for you.'

'From what I've heard of him,' Mr Gordon said, 'he wanted to use the travelling time dictating his instructions for further actions into a midget recorder while the meeting's fresh in his mind. I'll find them relayed on to my answering machine in the morning.'

Jill had hoped to sneak into the house but her parents, who usually adhered to farmers' early hours, were in their dressing gowns and ready for bed but lingering over a last cup of tea. Her mother almost dragged her into the kitchen, sat her down and poured an unwanted mug of tea. 'You *must* tell us what's going on,' she insisted.

'No need to panic,' Jill said. 'I haven't gone on the streets.'

Mrs Allbright snorted indignantly. 'We never thought for a moment that you had. But we're always concerned for you and when you suddenly change your hours and leave mysterious notes and come home with a lot of expensive new clothes...'

'I haven't got myself a sugar-daddy either.'

'Don't bother listing all the things you haven't done,' her father said mildly. 'We could be here until Doomsday. Why not just tell us what's happened?'

'All right,' Jill said. 'I'll tell you.' In fact, she had been awaiting the most suitable opportunity to gloat aloud over the story of the chances which had led to her change of fortunes, but some inhibition had told her that to pour out the story without being pressured for it would smack of boasting, a habit which her parents had drummed out of her before she entered her teens. She began at the beginning and told it all. If, perhaps, she laid undue emphasis on her own brilliance and initiative, she might be forgiven. When, at last, she came to the end, there was silence for a full half-minute.

'You may as well go to bed,' her mother told her severely, 'if you're going to make up a lot of fairytales.'

Five

Jill had been riding the crest but now she began to question her luck. She entered several days of mental turmoil. She was plagued by a recurrence of unanswerable questions. *Why me? Is this real? Has somebody at last perceived my true worth? How long will it be before I blow it or they see through me and cast me into outer darkness?*

But there was little time for self-doubt except during rare wakeful periods in the night. All the concentration that she could muster was needed to meet and rise to each fresh challenge. The task of slotting herself into the company structure was made more difficult by the vagueness of her remit and the understandable suspicion of her colleagues about the arrival of an unknown with an extraordinary introduction.

On the morning after her hectic first day, she was again half surprised to be admitted to the building at all. She was at her desk early, insulated in her own – her very own – office, yet aware of the sounds of people arriving, of lifts, of doors, of footfalls. She tried again to digest the company bible and was beginning to detect a network of logic in the baldly expressed managerial edicts, but she was interrupted by the delivery of a mobile phone of astonishing complexity. She had hardly begun to dip into its instruction booklet (which appeared to have been translated literally from the Japanese by someone whose acquaintance with English was limited to technical jargon) when she was interrupted again by a girl from the post room. This young lady, who was plain, very spotty and wearing jeans into whose denim the contours of her intimate anatomy had been conspicuously abraded, seemed perturbed to find that the in-basket was already occupied by the stack of files which Jill had still to read. She compromised by balancing several loose documents on top of the pile.

These turned out to be internal memos, the first two being from Mr Gordon. In the first, he confirmed that the union had already accepted the offer of five per cent and the depot would be fully functional again by that afternoon. In the second, he explained rather stiffly that he had known about the strike and of the pipeline contract, but since nobody had seen fit to inform him of the shipload of piping he had not been aware of any abnormal urgency connecting the other two events.

At this point there was a cursory rap on the door and Sheila Dobson entered. It seemed to Jill that even the interruptions to her interruptions were subject to interruption.

'Good morning, Miss Allbright. I hear that you had a fun evening.'

This was a whole new dimension. 'What are they saying?' Jill asked.

Sheila's formal manner fell away and she produced her ready grin. 'From what I hear, Herb Spicer's out on bail and trying to get up a lynch mob but the others won't go along with him. And somebody said that you talked the strikers into going back to work and the top brass are thinking of putting up a statue in your honour.'

'That's rubbish. But what do the staff think?'

Sheila shrugged. 'They're not thinking yet, they're just reacting. A sort of envy, mostly, and wondering what effect this cat will have among the pigeons.' Her face sobered. 'You don't mind me talking like this?'

'I insist on it,' Jill said. 'I have a tough row to hoe. For God's sake keep me in touch with what people are saying.'

'All right. Mr Fiddich would like a few words with you.'

Jill thought swiftly. Her first contact with

the General Manager might set the tone for the future. If she walked into Mr Fiddich's room, she would be giving him the opportunity to keep her standing in front of that big desk, establishing an inappropriate dominance over the representative of the two Messrs Hochmeinster. Equally, to seat herself uninvited might be to get off on the other, but just as wrong, foot. Better to put the ball back into his court. 'Any time that suits him,' she said. 'I'll be in for most of the morning. You'll have to introduce us.'

Sheila twinkled at her, two girls together against the enemy, and turned to leave.

'Another thing,' Jill said. She picked up the mobile phone. 'I'll have to learn these instructions some day but, to save time, do you know how to program numbers into this damn thing?'

Sheila took the mobile phone. 'Jot down the numbers you want loaded, in the order that you want them, and I'll get somebody to do it for you.'

'Thanks. And would you phone James and French for me, the auditors? I want an appointment with somebody senior who had some responsibility for the last company audit.'

'Can do.'

'Last thing. Remember, with gossip it's better to receive than to give. You bring me what you hear but you do not tell tales about me. Right?'

Sheila winked, mimed zipping her mouth, made a sign of the cross over her heart and withdrew.

The next memo was from George Wallis, the Depute Engineering Director. He conveyed the impression of being cut to the quick by any suggestion that he might have neglected his duty. He had known that the shipload of pipes was on the way but had not been told about the strike.

Sheila appeared again, this time opening the more regular door. 'Miss Allbright, Mr Fiddich,' she said solemnly. 'Mr Fiddich, Miss Allbright.'

Jill had previously only glimpsed Mr Fiddich as a distant figure. He turned out to be a round and rosy man with close-clipped white hair around a perfectly circular, red bald patch. Seeing him close to, Jill realized that he was no more than fifty and that the impression of great age stemmed from the network of fine lines texturing skin which was also heavily spattered with freckles. His manner was fussy and harassed, matching his telephone voice, but he shook Jill's hand politely and welcomed her into the company with apparent sincerity, managing to suggest that he was condescending to pay an impromptu call on a valued subordinate.

He seated himself with due care for perfect creases.

'Well, now,' he said, 'we seem to have resolved last night's crisis very satisfactorily.'

The assumption that he had made any contribution whatever to that resolution almost took Jill's breath away, but as he chatted on she realized that he was only emphasizing defensively, in mitigation of any earlier laxity, that he was now au fait with all the later developments. The pipe-shifting operation was almost finished, quantities were being checked, the financial details were being settled and the disposition of the pipes was being woven into the longer-term planning for the pipeline.

Jill expressed satisfaction without being specific as to whose performance was so impressive. 'Mr Hochmeinster will want to know how the crisis was allowed to arise in the first place,' she pointed out.

'I'm making my own enquiries,' he said stiffly. 'I'll let you know my conclusions.'

Jill felt a momentary spurt of resentment at being forced into confrontation with much older and more experienced staff. His conclusions would not be wanted as much as his excuses. 'Perhaps it may be considered a little unwise to have gone off to London with such a crisis looming,' she suggested.

His rubicund face darkened further. 'I expect my staff to liaise on such things. I shall certainly have something to say about inter-departmental communication at the next senior staff meeting.'

One of Jill's tutors had been explicit and she recalled and paraphrased his words. 'You have the overview. I would have expected you to check that everything was in hand.'

'I can't be expected—' He broke off. 'Miss Allbright, I really do not expect to face criticism from a depute who has only been with the company for a matter of hours.'

Jill was suddenly aware of her own heart-beat. 'Mr Fiddich,' she said, 'I am not your depute.'

He waved an airy hand. 'As good as. You're in my depute's room and on the appropriate salary grade. I checked.'

'Perhaps you should have checked a little further.' She looked at the next of the slips of paper in front of her and absorbed the previously only glimpsed words. 'You may not have read your morning's mail yet, but according to this you are being advised that I am here as the representative of Head Office and in particular of Mr Hoch-meinster.'

'You are still a member of my staff!' Mr Fiddich intended to sound authoritative, Jill thought, but he merely sounded peevish.

Jill nearly backed down. She was too young, too inexperienced, they had no *right* to expect so much of her. But her innate stubbornness combined with her abundant common sense carried her onward. 'I don't think so,' she said. She glanced at her watch. 'Mr Benjamin Hochmeinster should be awake by now. I have his mobile number and he told me not to hesitate to use it, whatever the hour. Shall we ask him to clarify the point?' She pushed the telephone towards him.

There was a protracted silence.

'Perhaps later,' he said at last.

'For the moment, then, please accept that, when I ask a question, it is just my way of saying that Mr Hochmeinster wants to know the answer.'

Jill had tried to speak gently but it was as if she had slapped him. 'I see,' he said through pinched lips. He rose without another word and left the room. She heard his door slam.

Sheila tapped and came through the connecting door. 'I've put your phone on charge. Someone from Services will come and give you a short course on the cellphone this afternoon. And Mr French of James and French will expect you around eleven thirty. They have their own car parking in front of their building. Unless you'd rather that he came here?'

'No, I'll go to him. He didn't quibble at giving time to a member of staff he'd never even heard of before?'

'He didn't seem at all surprised.'

Jill looked at her cheap digital watch. A better, more showy watch would have to figure on her shopping list. 'I'll have to leave in a few minutes.' She became aware that her mouth was dry. 'First, would you get me a cup of coffee from the machine?' She fumbled for coins.

Sheila's tip-tilted nose turned up. 'We do rather better than that up here. I'll fetch you a cup.'

Jill read another memo. Mr Brown, the Logistics Director, had been advised about the shipload of pipes but the arrangements had been in the hands of Head Office. Nobody had seen fit to advise him of the strike. Jill's impression was that he was secretly pleased that planning from which he had been excluded had gone seriously agley.

Sheila returned within a few minutes, bearing a cup of coffee which, although indisputably instant, was definitely superior to that dispensed by the machine. There was also a cream biscuit. Jill began to feel at home. Nevertheless, one delicate subject

92

had to be broached. 'Perhaps I should push for my own secretary,' she said.

Sheila pretended to bridle. 'I've hardly had time to prove myself incompetent,' she pointed out.

'It's not that. I'm sure that you can type ten thousand words a minute while writing shorthand with your toes. It's a question of divided loyalties. I've just had a word with Mr Fiddich.'

'I heard,' Sheila said. 'I wasn't listening, but this partition's thin and there's a gap under the door.'

'Then you'll understand. There could come a time when Mr Fiddich tells you to keep me in ignorance about something. But if I'm to do my job, it's vital that secrets aren't kept from me. You might prefer not to be put in that position.'

The secretary thought for a few seconds. Her face, for once, was serious. 'If Mr Fiddich wanted to fire me for disobeying that order, would you support me with Head Office?'

'Yes. But I certainly wouldn't go out of my way to let him know how I came to be so well informed.'

Sheila's smile came back. 'That's all that I wanted to know,' she said.

The offices of James and French occupied a

pair of towering semi-detached Victorian houses to the west of Union Street, supplemented by an extension into the large gardens at the rear. At the front, much of the garden space had been covered with tarmac and was now occupied by cars ranging from the new and medium-priced to the distinctly plushy. Slotting her 'old banger' into a space reserved for visitors, Jill made up her mind to investigate the company's car-loan scheme before her image suffered a permanent stain. She tidied her hair before leaving the car.

The granite front reared up for four tall storeys. Through basement windows, she could see staff poring over papers or VDUs. One of the twin front doors was screened by plants in tubs, but inside the other she was gathered up by a cheerful youth in a grey coat and escorted to Mr French's room. This, to judge by the size, the bay windows and the elaborate cornices, had been a drawing room in the house's heyday. It was now furnished in a manner which combined the businesslike with dignity and comfort, far divorced from the functionality of the basement offices. It was a step up, even from the impressive office of Mr Fiddich, and Jill took mental notes of the decor and furnishings against the day when she might aspire to such a room.

Mr French – Andrew French, as he introduced himself – was a well-dressed and
well-preserved man who must have been
nearing the age for retirement. His figure
had remained trim and though his face was
lined and changed by the years, he had kept
such a head of dark hair, only slightly
flecked with grey, that Jill took a secret
glance, suspecting a toupee. But no, the hair
was his own even if the colour might have
received a little assistance. All in all, she was
thankful that she was wearing her new
business suit. She had been transported into
a sphere in which expensive grooming like
Mr Benjamin's was far from unique. She
made up her mind to subscribe to some
suitable magazine in preparation for some
serious shopping.

Ignoring the large desk with its computer
and disciplined groups of papers, Mr
French settled them in two of the low armchairs around a gleaming coffee-table and
asked Jill what he could do for her.

'It's good of you to see me so quickly,' Jill
said.

Mr French smiled and made a dismissive
gesture. His smile turned his face from an
undistinguished assembly of features into
an aspect of charm. Then it was gone again.
'Even if I had not known your father – I was
his accountant when he owned Cairncarry

Farm – I could hardly do less for the new – um – whiz-kid on the block.'

Jill was startled. 'Is that what I am? A whiz-kid?'

'Didn't you know? That's the word that's going around. The North Sea oil industry is very concentrated around here. News spreads faster than light and I'm rather well placed to gather it. An ear to the ground can sometimes put an auditor on the track of something that wouldn't show up in the figures. The strike at the Oltech depot with a ship due in was big news and a prime topic of discussion – and not a little malicious amusement among Oltech's rivals. So, naturally, when a very expensive fiasco was deftly averted by a totally unknown member of staff, it was no surprise when you were seen being wined and dined by Mr Hochmeinster Junior. This morning, we learn that the strike was settled. No doubt the industry will soon be buzzing with rumours about your new responsibilities.'

'Accurate rumours?' Jill asked.

Mr French smiled again and shrugged. 'Rumours in the oil industry – as opposed to scandal – usually turn out to be very near the mark, except for the occasional one deliberately started as an exercise in misinformation.'

Jill tucked away the thought among her

mental files. 'Mr Hochmeinster Senior wants me to act as his personal assistant over here,' she said. 'That much, I suppose, will soon be public knowledge. Can we keep the rest of this between ourselves?'

'Of course.' Watching his eyes, Jill decided that she could trust his discretion.

Jill's remit had been to check on the competence of James and French, but her father had vouched absolutely for Andrew French's competence and honesty. She chose her words carefully. 'Mr Hochmeinster has been worried about the British operation. It's nothing that he can put his finger on yet, but the whole operation seems shaky. It isn't as smooth as it should be, or as profitable. They were thinking of putting in an American manager, but that might not do the trick if he goes in cold. First, they want somebody with fresh eyes and local contacts to take a good look around and ... and see what's going on. I don't know why they should pick on me—'

'Perhaps,' Mr French said, 'you were the first local to show up as having some initiative and no axe to grind.'

Jill digested the comment before going on. 'Benjamin Hochmeinster suggested that I contact you.' That was more or less the truth. She decided to fish for more guidance. When Mr French remained silent she said, 'What's your own feeling?'

He chuckled. 'Auditors are seldom asked for impressions,' he said. 'Perhaps they should be. Auditors can sometimes see a little deeper than the figures produced to them. In the case of Oltech UK, the figures were perfect. A bad auditor may do little more than check the vouchers and the arithmetic. We went much deeper than that, comparing every figure that we could lay hands on. We even found one or two minor fiddles on expenses. One engineer, for instance, took his car over to Norway by ferry for a tour of investigation around the rig maintenance yards and included the mileage across the North Sea and back again.'

'So you conclude that everything's above board?' Jill asked.

Andrew French looked sharply at her. 'I don't conclude anything, one way or the other. You asked to speak in confidence. Now I ask you to keep anything I say between ourselves. You'll do that?'

'I promise. Always assuming,' Jill added quickly, 'that what you tell me doesn't turn out to be something that it would be wrong to keep from my employers.'

'Nothing like that; but I wouldn't want it bruited abroad that I pass on my intuitions. I can't offer you any facts. An auditor isn't thanked for producing hunches or working by intuition – he's not in the business of starting scares and scandals. But since Oltech took over Shennilco, the organization has a different feel to it. I suppose you know that policy decisions are now made from Florida?'

'I know. That seems to have started the rot.'

'There's little doubt about it.' He settled back in his chair and put his fingertips together. 'That kind of downgrading has a predictable effect on an organization. Morale suffers. Individuals may still do their jobs but management slackens. Individuals feel slighted and less secure, so they start weighing their actions in the light of what's good for themselves rather than for the firm. It didn't help that the previous General Manager's health broke down and he had to take early retirement.'

Mr French paused.

'And,' Jill suggested, 'Mr Fiddich hasn't turned out to be quite the ball of fire he was expected to be?'

'Quite so. I hate to speak ill of anybody with whom I had a moderately good relationship while he was in his previous post but, frankly, responsibility has turned the man into a pompous ass. So it's difficult to know and not my job to speculate whether the downturn in profits is due to incompetence, bad luck or ... something less savoury.'

Jill took time to think that over. 'But surely,' she said at last, 'if there's a fraud going on, it's the auditor's job to spot it.'

'Not necessarily. I see that I shall have to give you my short course in peculation.' He glanced at his watch. 'I would offer to give it to you over lunch, but I have an engagement. So it will have to be a very short course, with a postgraduate version to come at a later date.

'Nothing is certain, but I think we can rule out simple embezzlement, firstly because we would almost certainly have spotted it and secondly because embezzlement is usually, though not always, quick. An embezzler may sometimes get away with it for years but he or she can't count on sloppy auditing, so it's usually a case of snatch and run.

'The next point is that we were only appointed to audit the British organization. An American firm audits the accounts in Florida and yet another firm does the audit of Oltech's operations in Malaysia. Large sums pass to and fro and, given collaboration between dishonest staff members on both sides of an ocean, it would be much less difficult to dip into the till.

'Again, if a member of staff is accepting bribes, no audit of the firm's books would show that up.'

'Bribes?' Jill said sharply. 'Bribes to do what?'

Mr French shrugged. 'You name it. To disgorge confidential information about tenders or geological surveys. To give a favourable decision in a dispute with a sub-contractor. To overlook substandard work by the same subcontractor. And while we're on the subject of bribery, I would hardly be allowed to audit the slush fund, which is anyway illegal.'

'There's a slush fund?' She had to hold her voice down.

'I'd be surprised if there wasn't, but there was not the least sign of it in the accounts.'

'How—?'

'How is it funded? Probably by the sale of some valuable equipment and writing it off as lost overboard from a rig or supply vessel. We checked the equipment and materials in use and in store but there is no way to search the bottom of the North Sea for valves and drill bits.

'The final point I feel I should make to you is the possibility of a covert, hostile plot. Oltech seems to have suffered a number of instances of bad luck and consequent bad publicity lately. Some rival company may be mounting a dirty tricks campaign.'

'With what motive?' Jill asked.

'I could only guess. But with new sections to the west of Shetland coming up for tender shortly, somebody might well want to damage Oltech's reputation and to make it difficult for Oltech to tender competitively. Any suggestion that Oltech cuts corners in matters of safety or environmental pollution might well have a bearing on the awarding of licences to develop new sections.'

Mr French looked at his watch again. 'I must leave very shortly for what promises to be a boring but ultimately remunerative lunch. I hope I've given you some food for thought.'

'Have you ever!' Jill said. 'I'm grateful.'

'I might not have been so outspoken, except that I remember you, running around your father's farm, when you were about twelve. A coltish tomboy with a mane of fair hair and permanently grazed knees. I'm delighted to see that your knees have made such a good recovery, by the way.

'I did my best for your father, but he had a large bank loan for renewing the farm buildings, brucellosis caught him at a bad time and the liquidation of J. C. Holland put the kibosh on it. I showed him a possible way to survive his difficulties but your father, perhaps rightly, decided that it might be legal but would certainly be dirty treatment of his own creditors. An honourable man is at a disadvantage in the world of finance. Give him my regards.'

Jill spent the afternoon at her desk. She found a new laptop computer awaiting her, still in its box. She took time to familiarize herself with its applications and specific oil-industry programs. She underwent instruction in the use of her new mobile phone and then worked her way through most of the emails, files and papers which had piled up for her attention, even committing the more important features to her memory, while managing to consider and digest what Andrew French had told her.

The continuous jumping from subject to subject was exhausting. She left for home with the feeling that her mind was clogged with a surfeit of new facts and surmises. On the way, she pulled her car out of the traffic and into a layby. Her new cellphone, charged and programmed, was in her new handbag. She was still in awe of Mr Benjamin but he had been sympathetic and more than helpful, and at least he was the devil she knew. His father had been an appreciative voice on the phone but he was still an unknown quantity. She keyed in the two digits and within seconds Mr Benjamin's voice came on the line.

'I've had a discussion with Mr French of James and French,' she said. 'And I've taken another opinion. They seem to be sound and trustworthy. He suggested certain lines to follow up. But I want to ask you something. The American, the British and the Malaysian operations are audited separately. Does anyone check up on the overall picture?'

'We call in all the accounts and a fourth firm does an overall audit.'

Jill felt deflated. 'Oh. I'm sorry if I've wasted your time.'

'Not at all. You've done well to get so far in so little time.'

Jill nerved herself. 'Then let me try to get a little further. I don't know who I can trust. How would you react if I suggested that you send over a computer expert to work with me?'

'I would ask what you wanted him for,' Mr Benjamin said cautiously.

'I want him to do some computer hacking. More than anything else, I want to have a look into certain bank accounts.'

'That would be highly illegal and the company would never countenance anything of the sort.' Jill was about to burst into apologies when he went on. 'However, as it happens I was thinking about sending one of our younger technicians over shortly.

There have been certain glitches in the software that he could look into. If he has time to spare, you may be able to find a use for him. He's offshore at the moment, but he could be with you in a week to ten days. I'll keep you posted.'

And this, Jill thought as she drove on towards home, was the man who had told her that he never meant more or less than what he said.

Six

The next day, the Thursday, Jill spent in the office – the new perspective on which, so alien at first, was becoming almost familiar. It was no longer a place for cleaning and polishing but somewhere where she had to participate, to watch and to learn.

Apart from her management course in the OU, her reading for nearly a year had been exclusively for pleasure, but the ability of the student to absorb from the page came back quickly. She would have been content to spend the day working through the accumulated papers on her desk as well as a growing number of emails. It proved to be a case of one step forward, two steps back. She had only reduced the pile on her desk by a finger's thickness when the young woman with the spots and the outrageously imprinted jeans topped it up again. Then Mr Ridley from Accounts, arrived bearing a much thicker bundle. He was a tall young man with a slightly horselike face and a generous but neatly trimmed crop of light brown curls.

'I come bearing rich gifts,' he said. His smile showed teeth which were not quite too straight. 'My chief, Mr Dalbeigh, had a fax from Miami. You're to have a copy of the latest accounts, as audited, and here it is. What on earth do you want it for?'

'I don't know that I do particularly want it. Let's say rather that Miami wants me to have it. How did Mr Dalbeigh react?'

'He just gave me the fax and told me to get on with it. But my guess would be that his hackles were up. He's inclined to think of the audited accounts as being nobody's business but his own.'

Mr Ridley lingered to offer advice on how to interpret the accounts and he continued to linger until she was quite sure that she was being 'chatted up'. She was also sure that Mr Ridley might be another who rather fancied himself, but not wholly without cause. He was not without a certain calculated charm.

'I'll have to go,' he said suddenly. 'But perhaps I can help a little more. May I offer you lunch?'

Jill took a few seconds to consider the proposition. Her impression was that to Mr Ridley a job was a job and that he had no more loyalty to the company than a mild gratitude for his monthly cheque. He might

107

prove to be a useful channel into the inner workings of the organization.

Ridley misinterpreted her brief hesitation. 'We could choose somewhere out of the way, if you preferred.'

That had all the makings of a Bad Idea. 'Quite the contrary,' Jill said. 'If we happened to be seen lunching together in some secluded hideaway, it would give exactly the wrong impression. I'll be happy to accept your lunch, but somewhere very open.'

He nodded seriously. Jill gathered that he had no objection to be seen on friendly terms with the attractive new mystery whizkid. 'Quite sensible. There's a canteen, but senior staff, those who don't go home, usually cross the road to the Marr Roadhouse.'

'And no strings,' Jill said.

'Of course not.'

She laid the accounts aside for more leisurely study and tried to go back to more immediate subjects. But her mind now refused to settle. Her attention had been caught by the cars in the office car park that morning. Oil company executives might be well paid – Mr Benjamin had said so – but Jill, despite or perhaps because her driving was confined to an 'old banger', sometimes scanned the motoring supplement in the *Press and Journal*, and she had a good idea what a top-of-the-range or even a mid-range car by one of the better makers cost.

Sheila Dobson, when consulted, told her that car loans were approved by the Personnel Director before being actioned by the Finance Director. She phoned Mr Gordon to ask whether he would be free if she came down, but was assured that he would come to her immediately. She guessed that he still felt vulnerable over the strike at the depot and needed to ingratiate himself with anyone who had the ear of either Mr Hochmeinster. Keep him that way, she decided.

When Jim Gordon joined her, she plunged in. 'It seems,' she said, waving a vague hand over some completely unrelated papers, 'that you were the first to get news of the strike. You must have known that the depot manager was away and his stand-in was off sick?'

Mr Gordon seemed to flinch. 'Yes, of course.'

'But you decided not to tell any of your colleagues?'

'They had already left for their homes. I decided to tell them in the morning. As I explained in my memo, I had no idea that the matter was urgent.'

'The shipload of pipes was not mentioned in the company newsletter?'

The Personnel Director's anxious face showed consternation. 'I ... I don't think so.'

Jill had already looked back through the newsletters and found a brief mention, but she would save that weapon for later use. 'We'll have to take a look,' she said kindly. 'Now tell me about the car-loan scheme.'

'Ah yes.' Mr Gordon seemed relieved to return to familiar ground. 'I was going to call it to your attention. You seem to be over-due for an upgrade.' Loans, he said, were available at a rate of interest which even Jill could see was very reasonable, and repayment was deducted from salary. So perhaps the possession of luxurious transport might not be a sign of ill-gotten gains. But as the conditions were explained, her management course came to her rescue again.

'Let's see if I understand this,' she said. 'The rate of interest is initially cheap but the interest payments remain constant for the duration of the loan?'

'Correct.'

'So the interest which is charged along with the last payment is at a rate which is in fact infinite?'

'That depends whether you consider the interest to be taken before or after the final payment, but in general that's correct.' Jim Gordon looked at her with new respect. Not many staff were so quick to see that the loans were not as generous as they might seem. 'For that reason, despite the tax implication, some staff prefer to have a leased company car. That might suit your circumstances. You would be taxed on it, but after two years you could purchase it at a much-reduced price. If you've looked after it, that can be a good bargain. Would you have any particular model in mind?'

Jill had been looking at the question of car purchase as a measure of the affluence of her colleagues, with only a distant yearning for benefit to herself; but with his words a whole new world opened up. For a moment, she saw herself in command of an exotic sports car, driving swiftly to upmarket events in a headsquare or with her hair blowing in the breeze; but she remembered in time the scarcity of suitable weather in Scotland and that her home was on a farm and approached over half a mile of private road which had never been tarred and was subject, in bad weather, to rutting and potholes and to snow-drifts which the Local Authority considered to be none of its own business. 'It would have to be four-wheel-drive,' she heard herself saying, 'with a good ground clearance.'

'Range Rover? Shogun? Nissan Patrol?'

Jill could not see herself at the helm of one of those monsters. She was tempted to opt for one of the smallest 4 x4s, a Suzuki or a Daihatsu Terios, but compromised on a medium-sized, petrol-driven vehicle, colour immaterial just as long as it was not fire-engine red.

'If you're not concerned about the colour,' Mr Gordon said, 'they can probably supply it off the shelf. Leave it with me.'

'Happily. Two other things. Will you furnish me with a staff list, with home addresses and phone numbers? Just in case we have another emergency?'

'No problem.'

'And I'd like a list of current staff car leases and loans.'

The Personnel Director looked shocked. 'That information is confidential,' he said. 'It's personal to the individual. You yourself wouldn't wish the world and his wife to know how much you owe on your car.'

'Probably not,' Jill said.

Jill had visited the Marr Roadhouse some months earlier with a party celebrating the engagement of two of her former fellow students. She liked it. The decor was more tasteful than the norm for such places, the service was almost prompt, the music was subdued and the food, considering its quality, was not overpriced.

Lunch with Mr Ridley passed off well. She

chose modestly priced dishes and only a half-pint of shandy to drink, which seemed to please and relieve him. As was proper in view of her seniority, he invited her to call him Kenneth but made no attempt to address her informally. He gave her some more insight in how to evaluate the accounts. He gossiped amusingly about the activities of the company. About his colleagues he was more reserved and carefully avoided any trace of malice, but Jill judged that this was no more than initial caution. When he came to trust her, he would open up.

The only task disrupting routine at the moment, he said, was the preparation of tenders for the new sections about to be opened up to the west of Shetland. This was the cause of much head-scratching, because the company had been only partially successful during the previous round of tendering, the most promising sections going to Oltech's bitter rivals, Omulco, so that two of Oltech's rigs and a platform were now mothballed in the Dornoch Firth and another rig was leased to Mobil. The final figures, he said, would be for the Board to decide.

'What's all the head-scratching about?'

Mr Ridley shrugged. 'Engineers not agreeing and two surveys contradicting each other, all as usual.'

She laughed. 'That's the story of an engineer's life. How often does the Board meet?'

'Monthly. But it meets in Florida.'

'There's one more thing,' Jill said. 'I'd like to have a list of the car loans and leases. On a disk, preferably.'

Mr Ridley promised. He seemed to think it natural that an unattached young lady might be interested in the finances of the car-owning members of staff.

She thanked him politely for the lunch. Next time, she said, it would be on her; but she left the date open.

She managed an afternoon of solid reading with only one interruption. This was the first call to come in on her new mobile phone. It took her several seconds to identify the unfamiliar tone and several more to remember how to answer the call.

The gruff tones of Mr Hochmeinster Senior came through clearly. 'How are you, young lady?'

'I'm very well,' Jill said.

'Settling in?'

'Yes.'

'Good.' That seemed to be sufficient time spent on necessary courtesies. 'Can you swim?' he asked.

It seemed a strange question but at least it was a straight one. 'I'm a strong swimmer,' she said. Mr Benjamin's words about being thrown in off the deep end came back into her mind but its relevance evaded her.

'Good,' he said. 'I want you to do the Off-shore Survival Course. I may need you to visit a rig. I'll get back to you.'

That evening, Jill made a point of being one of the first to leave the office, but she sat for a while in her car, parked inconspicuously in a corner. She was watching to see who got into the larger and newer cars. A later comparison with the list of car loans might prove informative. Some of the faces were unfamiliar to her, but she told herself that she would recognize them again.

Her new situation, she found, was begin-ning to seem less like a rather wild fantasy and more as though it might some day come to feel comparatively normal. She arrived home in a mood of returning confidence.

Over the evening meal, her mother said, 'You haven't told us much about the new job, dear. What are you actually doing?'

'And what do they call you?' her father added. Job titles, he knew, were important clues.

'I suspect that they're calling me all sorts of names behind my back,' Jill said, 'but at the moment I seem to be the local dogsbody for the big chiefs in Miami.'

'I hope they're paying you properly,' said her mother.

'They're paying me very well,' Jill said. 'In fact, I was going to give you a cheque for my share of the housekeeping.'

'No need for that. Not until you get on your feet.'

'You can take it that I'm on my feet now.' Jill's bonus had just reached the bank and she had received written notice of her salary. The deposit slip and the memo were burning a hole in her pocket. She nearly produced them to emphasize her independence but changed her mind. There are some things that a girl does not tell her mother. Her exact income is first on the list.

Jill lunched alone in the Marr Roadhouse on the Friday. She recognized several faces from the Oltech office and attracted some speculative glances from the younger staff, but was evidently considered too dangerous to approach. One young man shot his cuffs, straightened his tie and seemed about to head in her direction with obviously predatory intent, but a word from one of his colleagues changed his mind for him. The word going around seemed to be that she was too hot to handle.

Back in her office, Jill was beginning to contemplate with satisfaction the almost cleared surface of her desk and the nearly empty in-basket when Sheila Dobson tapped and entered and laid a copy of an outgoing letter in front of her. 'You may want to discuss this with Mr Fiddich,' she said. 'But you'll have to wait until Monday. He's just gone to chair the weekly meeting of senior staff.' She waited expectantly.

The letter seemed innocuous to the point of triviality, but then the real import of Sheila's words struck her. 'Where?' she asked.

'In the Board Room.'

'God bless you.'

Jill grabbed a pad, a pencil and, as an afterthought, the mobile phone which seemed to have become part of her personal accessories. She hurried to the opposite corner of the building and pushed through the double doors.

Her first impression was that the large room was filled with bald heads and probing eyes, some curious, some hostile, but some almost friendly. At second glance there were a mere dozen or so faces, some of them reflected in the long tabletop which she had polished so lovingly over the preceding months. There were several quite respectable heads of hair and, among the men, one plump, well groomed, middle-aged woman.

Mr Fiddich sat at the head of the table. Indignation was written all over his round, birdlike face. 'I'm not aware that you were invited to this meeting, Miss Allbright.'

Jill had come to expect occasional hostility and was learning to meet it head-on. 'Are you excluding me?'

The General Manager seemed taken aback at being challenged by a female, younger and his junior, but he raised his chin and produced a glare. 'Is there any reason why I shouldn't? You have made it clear that do not consider yourself to be a member of my staff.'

At the epicentre of an imminent upheaval, Jill activated her mobile phone and keyed in the two digits of Mr Benjamin's coded number. To her great relief, he answered immediately. 'Mr Hochmeinster? This is Jill Allbright,' she said. 'Mr Fiddich is holding a meeting of senior staff. He wants to bar me from it. What are your wishes?'

'Let me speak to him, please.'

Jill walked round the table and handed over her phone. Out of the corner of her eye, she saw that the faces in view were either concealing amusement or were calculatedly uninterested.

The General Manager listened for several minutes, interposing only a few truncated phrases. 'I'm sure you wouldn't ... But if you ... Yes ... Well, if that's what ... No, of course I...' He disconnected at last and handed back the phone. His face was stiff and his voice strained as he said, 'Mr Benjamin Hochmeinster would like Miss Allbright to sit in on our discussion. As an observer, you understand. Please take a seat, Miss Allbright, and welcome to the meeting. Let me introduce you.' With a gradual *volte face*, he had turned himself into a condescending superior.

Jill took one of several vacant chairs, placing herself beside one of the few faces she knew, Edward Brown, the Logistics Director. She nodded and smiled as the faces were introduced to her. She tried without much hope to memorize names and faces. The lady turned out to be Mrs Godleigh, the company solicitor.

As discussion resumed, Jill had more time to associate faces and responsibilities, knowing that names would follow.

The subject under discussion was the preparation of tenders for the licences for subsea exploration to the west of Shetland. The seismic survey, in the form of a printout of columns of figures stretching to many pages, was available and its representation in coloured-map form was on the wall. There were reports on the table. Edward

Brown obligingly shared his copies with Jill.

The engineering disciplines were represented by Malcolm McRobb, returned from his visit offshore, and his depute George Wallis. Mr McRobb was a hard-looking man with a seamed face and thinning hair. He was the only man present without a tie. There were many unknowns in the equations. The price of crude oil would be decided by OPEC, but the cost of extracting it was a matter, as Edward Brown disgustedly expressed it, of 'crystal ball and tealeaves', an opinion to which the engineers took exception. The Chief Accountant (a portly and silver-haired man with a strong Yorkshire accent who Jill already knew to be named Dalbeigh), supported by the Logistics Director, seemed to be arguing for conservative figures in order to give themselves a margin for unknown contingencies.

Others were arranged against them, arguing for a more adventurous approach lest the concessions be lost. Prominent in this camp were the Exploration Director and the Marketing Director. The latter, whose name Jill later learned was Dixon, was the very image of a Scotsman in the semi-fictitious Highland mould, having a curly red beard, a round face and a largely bald head. Below the neck, however, he was a disappointment, being rather lean and dressed in a suit of the very latest cut.

Between the engineers there was a rift. The Engineering Director expressed reservations about the seismic survey, which differed in several respects from an earlier gravity survey. His depute, George Wallis, however, when invited by Mr Fiddich to agree or disagree with that view, abandoned the depute's convention of 'my chief, for right or wrong' and took issue on this, pointing out that the earlier survey had been carried out using outdated technology and he was adamant that the figures could not lie.

Jill managed, with an effort, to follow the discussion, although it was strange territory to her. She tried to evaluate the personalities engaged. Her one conclusion was that Mr Fiddich, who had avoided expressing any strong opinions of his own, was an able administrator rather than a good manager, which might explain why he had looked good as a depute but had not shone from a more exalted level. When the debate began to become acrimonious, he called a halt.

'If Florida wants to make the decisions,' he said, 'let them do so. I'll draw up a report summarizing the options.' (A week later, Jill received a copy of a document which expressed the divergent views with admirable lucidity and invited a decision. No recommendation was made. She was already becoming tuned in to matters of management and felt sure that the lack of a positive recommendation would leave a definite black mark on Mr Fiddich if not on his team as a whole.)

Several minor items were disposed of and then Mr Fiddich arrived at the topic which had been Jill's prime reason for forcing her way into the meeting. 'It remains,' he said, 'to deal with the crisis arising from the sudden strike at the depot – a crisis which was only averted by the courageous action of Miss Allbright,' he added. The words, gracious in themselves, seemed to be forced out of him by an internal pressure. 'That crisis arose because certain members of staff each knew only a part of the overall picture, so I see no need to apportion blame. But we must prevent it ever happening again.' He went on to spell out procedures to ensure that staff kept each other informed. Which, Jill decided, was all very competent; but Mr Fiddich had managed to gloss over the fact that he had been the only person who should have had the overall picture very much in mind.

When the meeting was breaking up, Jill asked the Logistics Director if she might keep his copy of the seismic survey. Mr

Brown smiled accommodatingly. 'By all means,' he said. 'Keep anything you want. They're of no further interest to me. All that I ever want to know is what goes where, how much has been allowed for it and who I'm to blame when it can't be supplied and delivered within the budget.'

Jill found Kenneth Ridley, from Accounts, waiting in her office with papers concerning her induction into the pension scheme. Jill listened absently and signed wherever he indicated, but her mind was on the vastly larger matter of the forthcoming tenders. She would have to make an effort to achieve an understanding of the various calculations, but she would never be granted long enough periods undisturbed in the office. On the other hand, she was damned if she was going to haul an ever-increasing tonnage of documents to and fro with her.

She showed Ridley the paper copy of the seismic survey. 'You're the only computer nerd I've come across around here with access to the server,' she said. 'If I give you a blank floppy disk, could you make a copy of this seismic survey on to it?'

Kenneth glanced at the copy in Jill's hand to check that there was a computer reference printed at the head. 'No problem,' he said.

123

Jill might have gone on to explain but at that moment the girl with spots came in. There was a man below, she said. Something about a new car.

Jill made a lightning apology to Kenneth Ridley and left her room precipitately. The lift journey to the ground floor took less than half a minute but she fretted all the way down. At the desk was an incredibly handsome salesman with some papers to sign and the keys to her leased company car.

In a slot near the front door was the car itself. She spotted it as she crossed the threshold and uttered a silent, wordless prayer that the four-by-four in pale, metallic blue would be the one. Sure enough, the salesman – quite ordinary looking, now that she took a proper look at him – led her directly to what was obviously the most beautiful car in the world. It was pristine. The seats, still shrouded in polythene, had never been sullied by an alien bum. There was a good radio/cassette player. There was air-conditioning. Everything was electrical even to the door mirrors and the sun roof. There was remote locking.

The salesman spent ten minutes instructing her, exchanged the papers and manuals for her signature and then signalled to a colleague and was picked up. She was left alone with all that unsullied, glistening machinery, undoubtedly the most perfect vehicle in the whole car park. She would have stayed to gloat, but duty called.

An hour later she was, for once, among the first to leave the office. Other staff making a prompt start to the weekend seemed to be casting admiring glances at her new toy. The sun was shining as was only proper – surely the gods in control of the weather would never have the heart or the temerity to rain on her glowing vehicle. It was heaven to be in a car that smelled of new upholstery instead of her father's agricultural pursuits and hell to know that it did not yet belong to her. As soon as funds permitted, she would buy it – or something even better, if such existed. She transferred her cassettes and a few other possessions from the 'old banger' and tuned the new radio to her favourite channels.

Mr Benjamin would be expecting a report. She pulled in to the same layby and killed the radio. The time – lunchtime in Florida – should be convenient to him. Jill had only just begun her report when a juggernaut ground by, drowning out their voices.

'Where are you calling from?' he asked when the noise had died.

'From my car. I didn't want to be overheard.'

'Very sensible. Have the car checked for

bugs by the company's security firm every couple of weeks. Go on.'

Jill gave him a summary of the meeting. 'What conclusions have you drawn about Mr Fiddich?'

'I think he's a very able administrator. He's circulating very precise instructions, making it clear which departments have to be informed of each possible contingency, to make sure that no failure of communications like the one about the recent strike ever happens again.'

'And as a manager?'

In her euphoric mood, Jill might have treated Mr Fiddich with more generosity than he had shown to her, but this was a direct question and she knew where her loyalty lay. 'He shouldn't have let it happen in the first place,' she said.

'Quite right. Keep an eye on him for me. Goodbye.'

The call died on her. Jill raised her eyebrows. She waited for a generous gap in the traffic, gave the proper signal and drove on. Mr Benjamin had been unnecessarily curt. But perhaps he had been in a meeting, she told herself.

Her parents came out of the farmhouse to see who was arriving in the smart new car. Jill parked in a corner of the barn, protected from the tractor and machinery by a stack of pallets. The salesman had pointed out the catch for the bonnet. She raised it to inspect the spotless engine, the immaculate wiring, the gleaming filler-caps for topping up this and that which she would have to puzzle out later. 'It goes with the job,' she told her father casually.

'Useful sort of vehicle.'

'It is. But you have a Land Rover for carrying things around the farm.'

'I've let you drive my car,' he pointed out sadly.

'Not often. And just look at your car, then look at this one. If this was yours, would you let me drive it? Not on your life,' she answered for him. 'Tomorrow, you can drive me to the office – in your car,' she added firmly, 'and I'll collect the old banger. When I'm sure I've finished with it, you can have it back to keep chickens in.'

Seven

Jill was yearning to dally with the new car but she had no intention of taking it into the thickest Aberdeen traffic until it was as familiar as her own footsteps and thus as responsive as her own feet. Only in that way could she be sure of the right reaction if an emergency was forced on her. In addition, the 'old banger' might be less conspicuous for what she had in mind. No doubt whispers about her new status symbol had already circulated among the staff.

Her father dropped her off at the Oltech office. His first suggestion had been that they use the new car for the trip. 'We'd be more comfortable,' he pointed out.

'And by the time I got home, you'd have carried a few sheep or pigs and a straw bale through a quagmire in it,' Jill retorted. 'No, thank you very much.'

After driving the new leased car, every squeak, rattle and knock of the 'old banger', noises which had faded through familiarity, came through loud and clear. The brakes felt feeble and the steering heavy. The city centre was busy on a Saturday but she bagged the last vacancy in a multi-storey car park, forced her way through the Saturday shoppers and made a serious hole in her bonus money in the better clothes shops. She had an image to keep up. She missed the comfort of Mr Benjamin's acute eye but nevertheless thought that she had chosen well.

With her packages carefully stored on the back seat, she set off on the real business of the weekend. She had transferred Jim Gordon's staff list of names and addresses to a disk and on a street map she had marked the addresses of any staff who she considered senior enough to be capable of serious wrong-doing. As a starting point, she was looking for anyone who seemed to be living beyond his or her means.

As she worked her way out from the city centre, the first addresses were in the better class of tenement flats. Then came the granite-built room-in-roof detached and semidetached houses. Further out, she was into the areas of expensive modern homes where the new car would undoubtedly have been less conspicuous than the 'old banger'. Her suspicions were stirred when she saw, on the gravel beside the garage of Mrs Godleigh's modern bungalow, two opulent and shining Jaguars. While she watched, however, the company solicitor drove off in a travel-stained Mini and a young man began to polish the two big cars. The shape of the cars raised a question in her mind and the number-plates confirmed that the cars were around ten years old, neither new enough to be expensive nor old enough to be classic collectibles. Evidently, Mrs Godleigh had a son who was 'into' cars.

A few staff members had addresses out in the country. She stopped off at the farm to switch to the new car. Winter had suddenly relaxed its grip and spring was showing itself in warmth and garden flowers. The countryside was alive with lambs and new growth. Jill left the remaining houses for the next day and instead treated herself to a rural ramble in the new car with the windows and sunroof open and the smells of spring in the car. The radio treated her to suitably vernal music. It was good to be young and alive.

On Sunday, she left home early. George Wallis, the Depute Engineering Director, had an address in the expensive territory between Cults and Culter. This belonged to a positive mansion standing in some acres of manicured garden. A gleaming Daimler stood at the door, but Jill had only watched for a few minutes when an older man came out and stowed a set of golf clubs in the Daimler's boot. Jill used her mobile to call her mother who consulted the telephone directory for her. Sure enough, the subscriber's initials were not those of the engineer. Young George, it seemed, lived with his parents. His personal transport, she recalled, was an elderly but well maintained sports car.

Jill drove on. She inspected two converted farmhouses showing recognizable symptoms of DIY and two modest houses in small satellite towns without seeing anything significant. She consoled herself, as she parked the new car carefully beside the old and polished off an almost imperceptible layer of dust, with the thought that she had enjoyed a familiarization drive in the country and now had a better idea of the backgrounds of her various colleagues.

The story of the young cleaner who had answered a midnight phone call and successfully deputized for a billionaire company president an ocean away was too egregious to remain untold. The media, belatedly, had got hold of it and were demanding more. At a time of little real news, human interest was in demand. Jill's change of fortune was meat to them. A reporter tracked her to her home that evening, there were several phone calls and at the office next day the phone calls, faxes and emails became almost a deluge. Security protected her from personal confrontation and, aided by Jim Gordon, she issued a release giving the barest facts without any embellishment. The story, when it appeared, was accompanied by a photograph snatched by a press photographer as she hurried from car to office that morning.

She did not have to suffer such harassment for very long. She lunched in the canteen and when she returned to her office the faxes had been flying. Mr Hochmeinster Senior had put her name forward for the Offshore Survival Course. There had been a cancellation due to illness. No doubt some pressure had been attached to the Oltech application, because she was offered the vacated place on the course, starting the following morning.

Next day, Jill left home in the 'old banger' and enrolled at RGIT. The Offshore Survival Course lasted for four days. Half a day was spent at Montrose, where Jill learned firefighting. She was taught to feel her way around a burning building in breathing apparatus, using the backs of her hands to prevent clamping-on in the event of meeting anything electrical and bare. She was shown the right and the wrong ways to attack different categories of fire and was allowed to extinguish more than one artificial bonfire for herself. The rest of the course was devoted to other emergencies – evacuation from a rig or platform and, more particularly, practising escape from a drowned helicopter using a dummy helicopter body in a swimming pool.

It was an intensive, stressful period but it was not entirely filled with lectures and practical escapades. Evenings were free and Jill went home each night.

Most of the others on the course were strangers to her but there was one face which was almost familiar. The lanky young man with close-cropped curls had been at university with her although, being two years ahead of her, they had hardly met except to dance together once in the students' union – on which occasion he had trodden rather painfully on her foot. But that incident was long in the past and it was natural for them to drift together at the lunch table on the second day.

They introduced themselves afresh. David Banion had spent two years doing seismic surveying in Oman but was now with BP. 'I don't need to ask what you've been doing,' he said. 'Today's papers are full of you. Are the stories true?'

'They got the basic facts more or less

right, give or take a bit. The rest was embellishment or pure invention.'

'I guessed as much. All the same, you seem to have had the sort of lucky break that most of us only dream of. Did you know you were on the telly last night?'

'Really?'

'Yes. Only on the nonstop news on Sky, though.'

'Fame at last,' she said lightly. 'If you've been doing seismic surveying, would you be able to interpret some marine survey figures?'

'Probably. I might have difficulty. Marine surveys aren't done quite the same way as onshore ones – they tow an array of what they call "airguns" behind a vessel, trawling along the bottom. It may be a different world.'

It was a chance to learn some more about this strange new oily world. 'Tell me all about seismic surveying,' she said and, pleased to have such a rapt and attractive audience, David told her as much as he could, up to the point at which he would have had to dive from the broad outline into the mass of detail.

'But tell me this,' Jill said. 'Is it possible for two surveys to disagree? Could engineers seriously argue with each other as to whether one survey or the other was reliable?'

'I think they could,' David said. 'If the earlier survey had been done with outdated technology, that one could be unreliable. I'd go along with the later one, but not everyone would agree. There are still those who look on the new technology as newfangled rubbish.'

After the last lecture on the last day and when they had both been assured that they had passed the course, David said, 'It's been hard work, but worth it. Do you feel like painting the town?'

Jill met his eye. At university, despite the damage to her best pumps, she had rather fancied David Banion, but at the time he had been 'going steady' with a student of domestic science who had since, as Jill knew, married a quantity surveyor. 'The answer's a qualified maybe,' she said. 'What, in your mind, constitutes "painting the town"?'

'A meal. The theatre or whatever's on at the Music Hall. Unless you'd rather visit a casino?'

'I don't gamble,' Jill said. 'Except, very occasionally, on the Lottery. And then we go home to our separate beds?'

'If you insist.'

'I do. The rest of it sounds like fun, though. Are we still on?'

135

His smile illuminated his eyes. 'Yes, of course.'

She phoned home to give warning that she would be late and they went for a quick meal with wine. A romantic comedy was playing at His Majesty's Theatre and there were still a few seats available. They held hands companionably in the semi-darkness and laughed in the same places.

During the interval, they adjourned to the bar and found a secluded corner. 'Perhaps I shouldn't tell you this,' he said, 'you being on the staff of a rival body, but the wine must have loosened my tongue. The whisper is that Oltech are going to miss out in the next round of tenders.'

'Who told you that?' Jill asked sharply.

'Nobody in particular. Just, whenever the tenders are under discussion, somebody's likely to say that they've heard Oltech won't be in the running.'

'But how would anybody know such a thing? The tender hasn't even been decided yet.'

'Damned if I know. People, *en masse*, sometimes seem to act like a giant computer, each putting in some tiny fragment of knowledge and, without anybody quite knowing how, suddenly everybody just plain knows. That's how rumours start.'

Several days of thought devoted to the

proposition that there might be dark doings somewhere unspecified had caused Jill to suspect finagling in the most innocent of remarks. 'This isn't just a piece of disinformation, aimed at getting Oltech to price themselves out of the market?'

He shrugged. 'If it is, I don't know it. If it's any help, it seems to be genuinely believed. I'll see what more I can find out and I'll give you a ring. Or are we going to see each other again? I hope so.'

They saw the rest of the play and left the theatre together. 'I am definitely not driving a car tonight,' Jill said. 'I'll call a taxi. Can I drop you off?'

'If Bucksburn's on your way.'

It was. In the taxi, they kissed. Jill was rather breathless when David left the taxi but she was her usual self by the time she reached home.

When Jill returned to her office on the Friday morning, her first act was to leave the new car in the office car park and beg a lift from one of the junior staff. But the 'old banger' was no longer where she had left it. (It was later found on the Beach Boulevard, burnt out by joyriders.)

Her lift returned her to the office, where she was met by the sight of a stack of papers in her in-basket. But she had hardly settled in her chair when George Wallis, the Depute Engineering Director, burst in. He was in too much of a hurry to sit down but addressed her from the doorway. 'The faxes have been burning up the lines,' he said. 'There's a question been raised about safety on one of the rigs. I'm flying out there now. The chiefs say that you're to come with me. In future, I suggest that you keep a bag in your car, ready for sudden trips. Dash home, change into something suitable and I'll pick you up from there. You did get your Offshore Certificate? Bring it along. You'd better tell me where you live.'

Jill told him and drew a quick sketch-map. 'What am I going along for?'

'God knows. Experience probably.'

Or to keep me out of the way, Jill thought. 'All right,' she said. 'Will we be away overnight?'

'Probably not, but it's safer to assume that it could happen.' He hurried out.

Jill drove briskly home. Her mother was out. She changed quickly into jeans and a sweater, threw some spares and toiletries into a soft bag and added a more respectable dress rather than risk being caught out by circumstances. She had already been issued, for the Offshore Course, with a hard hat. She had also been given safety boots designed for more masculine feet so she added several pairs of socks.

She had time to use her mobile phone. Mr Benjamin answered. 'I've just been ordered offshore,' she said. 'Did that come from you or am I being shunted out of sight?'

'Those were Dad's orders. Somebody made a complaint to the Health and Safety Executive about safety on Caber Beta. It's not the first such occasion, as I think you know. We can't afford the usual company whitewash, we want to know if there's really been any risk and, if so, how and why, who told your HSE and why again, and what we're going to do about all of it.'

She caught her father dismounting from the tractor in the yard and explained. 'You are a dear good man,' she added severely, 'and I love you to bits, but if you even breathe on my car while I'm away I shall undoubtedly kill you.'

Her father's protestations of good intent were interrupted by the arrival of George Wallis in the sports car with the top down. Jill quickly donned her hard hat and got in. 'You don't trust my driving?' he asked.

She tapped the hat. 'I'd rather have my hair flattened than tied in knots,' she said.

Jill's first trip in a real, as opposed to a dummy, helicopter was an anticlimax. She had expected a scenic, birdlike trip but instead she was jammed in a crush of men in a noisy, bumpy cabin which was almost immediately out over a grey sea. After half an hour, a cluster of platforms came into view, each one a complex assembly of decks and machinery. The helicopter singled out one of them, settled, decanted Jill, George Wallis and a few other men and took off again.

By that time, at his suggestion, they were on first-name terms. Jill was learning the fine shades of convention in the company and, without quite liking him, she had calculated that she and George Wallis were of approximately equivalent seniority, so that such informality was acceptable. He seemed to know his way. He led Jill down metal stairs and along galleries and into the presence of the Offshore Installation Manager, a small but hard-looking man named Baxter. He had an accent which Jill pinned down as Australian or possibly New Zealand. They sat in surprisingly comfortable metal chairs. Around them, the platform was alive with orderly activity, sometime noisy and never quite silent. The predominant smells were of salt water and diesel.

'We're not supposed to know this,' Mr Baxter said, 'but I've had a friendly tip-off. The Health and Safety Inspector's on the way. Somebody's made a complaint. I don't know who and I can't think what about. Our safety checks, drills and procedures are up to date and we haven't had an accident in six months.'

'Then you should be bomb-proof,' George said. 'You'll be busy. Perhaps I could run over things with your Safety Officer before the Inspector gets here?'

'Surely. Remember, we're not supposed to know that he's coming. You're here about something else.'

'Right.'

The Safety Officer was a sallow man with a pronounced Glasgow accent. He and George, with Jill as an interested observer, repaired to his office and checked through systematic records of inspections. They ate a remarkably good lunch in an austere canteen and began a tour of alarm systems and fire-fighting and escape equipment. It was unfamiliar territory to Jill but everything looked sound and the two men seemed to be satisfied.

The approach of another helicopter interrupted them in inspecting a freefall lifeboat. They separated from the Safety Officer but met him again in the Offshore Installation Manager's room, where the Health and Safety Inspector had already arrived. Jill was pleased to recognize the visiting Inspector as a man who had given a lecture on the

Offshore Course.

'I represent the Aberdeen office,' George said, 'and Miss Allbright represents Head Office in Miami. We were here on a matter of stocktaking, but if there's any question of safety we'd like to be along.'

The Inspector looked twice at Jill. 'I've seen you before,' he said. 'You were on last week's course. Right?'

'Right,' Jill said.

'Well, now you'll see what it's all about. Let's get going.'

The three men, trailed by Jill, went over much the same ground as had been covered earlier. Then, 'Let's see your Incident Record,' the Inspector said.

They returned to the Safety Officer's small office. The book was produced. The Inspector seemed to know exactly what he was looking for. He put his finger on an entry. 'You had a fire,' he said.

'Is that what brought this on?' the Safety Officer asked.

The Inspector smiled and shrugged. 'No comment,' he said.

The Safety Officer sighed. 'It was a chip-pan fire. Not even a deep-fat fryer, an ordinary saucepan. One of the cooks was making himself some breakfast and the fat caught. It was a nothing but it was duly logged.'

'Show me the kitchen,' the Inspector said after a moment's thought. 'If it passes, I'll get ashore. When's the next chopper?'

'There's one almost due,' George said. 'We'll come with you, if there's room.'

'I want to meet the OIM again,' Jill said.

'It's the last chopper tonight. We'll have to stay over.'

'If we must.'

'Hell! I had a heavy date for tonight.'

'You can still have it. You don't have to stay for my sake.'

George thought about it but came to a reluctant decision. 'No, I'll wait. It wouldn't do to abandon you to the mercies of all these sex-starved roustabouts.'

'OK. One moment,' she said. She turned to the Safety Inspector. 'Can I have a private word?'

The Inspector looked surprised and even slightly shocked, but he said, 'I suppose so.' The other two men walked on.

Jill looked up, down and around but there was nobody within earshot. 'It seems to me,' she said, 'that you were brought out here on a fool's errand. Unless somebody's playing a practical joke on you, this was a piece of malice directed against the company. And not the first, right?'

'Perhaps.'

'Somebody probably thought that there

was a chance of a snap inspection turning up something more serious than a chip-pan.'

'I can't argue with that.'

'And somebody knew that there had been a chip-pan fire.'

'If you're working round to asking me who made the complaint, I'm not allowed to tell you.'

'You mean,' Jill said, 'that whistle-blowers, even malicious ones, are entitled to confidentiality. But would you care to confirm that it had to originate from somebody on board this platform?'

'I can't even comment on that,' said the Inspector, but he was nodding his head slowly.

The Offshore Installation Manager was busy but he could spare a few minutes for Jill and George. They had to wait until a meeting broke up. Three men filed out of the office. 'Geologist ... Directional driller ... Electronics boffin,' George whispered.

When they were admitted, Jill said, 'That visitation resulted from a malicious complaint.'

'It happens,' said the OIM.

'More than usual, lately?'

'Perhaps. Doesn't matter, as long as we're on the ball.'

'There's no harm done this time, I grant you,' Jill said. 'But if somebody seizes on every excuse to call out the HSE, the odds are that some day he'll spot something that's been overlooked. Right?'

'I hope not,' said the OIM, 'but it could happen.'

'This may be part and parcel of a more organized campaign. It seems to have originated with somebody who knew about the chip-pan fire three days ago.'

'That could be a lot of people.'

Jill took a moment for thought while the OIM tapped an impatient finger on his desk. 'These malicious acts,' she said, 'must originate somewhere and Miami wants them back-tracked. Have you any idea who might have leaked the information, direct to the HSE or through somebody else? Some-one with a chip on his shoulder?'

The OIM shrugged.

'Will you run me off a list of everybody who was on the rig from three days ago until the HSE got the complaint – say yesterday evening?'

'I'll do that.'

They had missed the last helicopter. George transferred to the support platform but there were cabins for the few women staff near the OIM's office. Jill slept lightly, disturbed by the constant, metallic bustle.

She woke once, her mind full of intelligent conclusions; but when she woke again to a noisy dawn she had forgotten most of them and the rest were rubbish.

Eight

George Wallis drove her home again from the airport. On the way, he made several half-heartedly suggestive remarks and then asked for a date, but Jill had little taste for his company and none for a romantic entanglement with him. She reminded him of the 'heavy date' which he had passed up the previous evening and declined the offer, but she kept it friendly. She could do without any unnecessary enemies within the company.

The media seemed to have forgotten about her but the stack of papers towering above her in-basket had not grown any less. Stifling the thought that her colleagues might be trying to keep her busy where she would be no threat, she buckled down, trying to absorb in short time the ongoing workings of a major oil company. She had managed to separate the urgent from the important and the important from the merely confusing, and was trying to segregate any items which might be relevant to her special responsibility, when she was interrupted by a polite knock.

The head which came round the door – at, she thought, a remarkable distance from the floor – was heavily freckled and blessed or cursed with a prominent nose, pale blue eyes and a crop of red hair which, being silky-soft, seemed ready to float in the breeze. It wore the sort of spectacles which were so old-fashioned as to have become highly fashionable. It raised its inconspicuous eyebrows.

'Come on in,' Jill said, trying very hard not to sound as though she wished every visitor a long way away.

The man came round the door. He was, as she had suspected, very tall and gangling. He was wearing jeans and a slightly tattered sweater. He shook her hand across the desk while still seeming halfway across the room. 'I'm Geoff Dubois,' he said. 'Did they tell you I was coming?' His voice was definitely American.

'I was offshore until a couple of hours ago,' she said. The words sounded good, almost boastful. She had become one of the elite. 'I expect there's a memo about it somewhere in this stack. What was it about?'

'Computers?' he suggested.

'Ah.' Jill bit off what he had been about to say. Walls, she remembered, were said to have ears. 'Perhaps we could have lunch?'

'Sure.'

'Give me a call about a quarter to one?'

'Sure thing.'

Within a few seconds of that time, he called her office number. They met at the front doors and walked out into cool sunshine. 'You won't have a car here?' Jill asked.

'Nope. I'm staying across the road. Not worth learning to drive on the wrong side.'

'Too many ears over there.' Jill led the way to her new car. She had no intention of leaving it parked in the city where it could be stolen or vandalized. She took her sunglasses out of the glove compartment and headed out of the city in the direction of a favourite pub. 'What did Mr Benjamin tell you?' she asked as she drove.

'It was the old man who briefed me. I'm over here to sort out a couple of bugs in the company programs but I'm to make myself available if you have any special, confidential requirements. I fly back in four days.'

'That doesn't give you much time for the bugs.'

'Hell, I could fix them in ten seconds if I wanted – they're the same ones I've fixed back at base. I'm spinning it out for whatever you're needing.'

'What I'm needing,' Jill said carefully, 'is a bit of hacking. Quite illegal. If you don't

149

want to stick your neck out, say so now.'

'I don't want to stick my neck out,' he said. Before Jill could react, he went on, 'But hacking wouldn't be sticking my neck out. I can do it so's no one can could ever trace it back to me. Laptop, mobile phone and route it through somebody else's server, then clean out the laptop. Leaves no electronic backtrack at all.'

As she parked the car, Jill decided that such a degree of quiet confidence would usually ring warning bells in the back of her mind; but his manner carried conviction. All the same, if the Flymo ever went over the dog turd, she would withdraw the hem of her garments.

The bar was moderately busy but they found a corner table where the neighbours on one side were a pair of businessmen talking golf and, on the other, four elderly ladies exchanging shrill scandal. Jill decided that it would be safe to speak freely. They ordered. Jill was content with cold meat and salad with a glass of white wine but Geoff, explaining that he needed calories to sustain him in the bitter climate, chose steak with all the vegetables and trimmings plus a pint of stout. Jill, who considered the spring day to be almost warm, made no comment.

When they had been served, she glanced at the neighbouring tables to be sure that the occupants were engrossed in their own trivia. 'There are signs,' she said. 'Things going wrong. Mr Benjamin wants me to watch for any disloyalty inside the company.'

'I guessed that from what little the old man told me.'

'If the worst comes to the worst,' Jill said, 'the company may have to bring in a big agency, do covert surveillance and phone-tapping, but that would cost a mint and almost certainly set off the alarms. It seems to me that there's more chance of finding out something you want to know if nobody else knows you're looking for it. Right?'

'That seems to figure.'

'I've been giving it some thought and I can only think of one way to finger anybody who's on the wrong side. If I'm wrong, tell me so. The one thing sure is that what's being done isn't just being done for fun or out of spite. It's too systematic for that. So somebody is being bribed. And what I want to know is whether anybody in the employ of the company has been getting richer than their salary would account for. Could we manage that?'

He nodded. 'Shouldn't be much of a problem.'

'But in four days?'

His glasses blinked as he nodded. 'I just

need to get private with the company computer and copy the payroll along with the numbers of the accounts that pay, expenses and overtime get paid into. And I'll want addresses and phone numbers.'

'I can give you that.'

'Right. Given that much, I can do the rest from the States. Probably cheaper than keeping me over here, the way your hotels charge.'

It seemed to Jill that he was making it sound too easy. 'But if somebody had a separate bank account overseas...'

Geoff nodded, shook his head and swallowed a quick mouthful of his steak, all apparently at the same time. 'If he has a different bank account, under a different name, uses a different password and PIN number and never accesses the account from his own phone or transfers money between accounts or makes a payment direct from the other account, then it might get tricky. Not impossible, but tricky. But nobody's that careful. All goes well for a year or two and they decide to do themselves a favour out of the easy money.' He looked at her seriously through his granny-glasses. 'Of course, if I find any unexplained deposits I'll leave it to you to find out whether it's dirty money, gambling wins or a legacy from an uncle, whatever.'

152

'Of course,' Jill said. 'If you can do that much, you'll have helped me halfway to my target. Tell me, when you get back to Miami, will they ask you how I'm doing?'

He shrugged. 'It would figure.'

'What will you tell them?'

His eyebrows went a surprisingly long way up. 'Hell, I haven't seen you in action except just now, but from what I've heard around the office...'

'Yes?'

'Mixed reactions. Some of the younger ones want to adopt you as a role model. The older guys are cagey in case you're after their blood or their jobs. Most of the men lust after you. And,' Geoff said with an extra flash of his glasses, 'you can definitely include me in that category. I suppose you wouldn't care to...?'

Jill looked at him and decided that he was joking. 'Not at the moment, thank you. What else?'

'That you're a tough lady and that you're on the ball. And how!'

Jill had a second date with David Banion that Sunday. The weather had turned hot. David collected her in his massive Volvo estate. Mrs Allbright, beaming benevolently, had provided the makings of a picnic for at least six people.

They drove up Deeside with all the windows open, crossed to the Don, left the main roads for rural by-ways and found their way to a hilltop. It was too early in the year for midges to bother them and there was a cooling breeze. They ate their picnic, or as much of it as they could manage, seated in the open tailgate of the Volvo. The rear seats had already been laid flat – for moving some furniture, David was quick to explain – and they soon found themselves relaxing on the carpeted floor and carrying on from where they had left off in the taxi.

They were young and healthy and they were attracted to each other. They were exchanging caresses of an increasingly permissive nature and might well have gone too far to retreat, except that they were disturbed by a sudden babble of voices. They pushed apart hastily and began to tidy their clothes. A skein of geese which had hardly bothered to climb for the hill passed low overhead, calling as they went and sounding like a chattering crowd. David tried to pull her down again. 'No,' she said breathlessly. 'It's too soon, too quick. And I couldn't relax, knowing that there could be a family of tinkers or a stalker with a telescope keeping an eye on us.'

'There's a roadhouse—' David began huskily.

'Definitely no.' Jill pushed him gently away. 'This is all going too quick and I'm not on for one-night stands.'

'You wound me. I wasn't thinking of a one-night stand. We could be so good together.'

'If you're looking to a slightly longer term, you can afford to be patient. Show me that you can be steadfast.'

'Yes. We'll see how we go, but you mustn't think that I'm afraid of a long-term relationship. Next time?'

Jill smiled in spite of herself. 'Maybe.'

'Dinner tonight? No strings.'

'I don't think so. I don't trust either of us. Without hurrying too much, take me home. And ask me out again soon.'

In the car, a silence fell between them. To break it he said, 'Two of the engineers were talking in the office the other day. They mentioned Oltech, which made me prick up my ears.'

'Why would it do that?'

'Because you work for Oltech.' He sounded amused.

'Now you're making me prick up mine,' Jill said. 'What was it about?'

'Nothing much. I really don't know why I mentioned it. One of them was saying that if they needed some drill collars in a hurry they could probably hire them from Oltech

155

and the other one said Oltech weren't in the business of hiring out equipment. How about the theatre tomorrow night?'

'Still too soon,' Jill said. 'Give me breathing space.'

When Jill arrived home it was to find her mother at the door and in a tearful fluster. 'Oh my!' was Mrs Allbright's greeting. 'We've had the police and I dinna ken who-all else. Aathing's tapsalteerie, I've naething ready for your tea and ... and...'

'Slow down, Mother,' Jill said. 'Never mind about tea, I've brought back enough of your sandwiches for a fortnight. Just tell me what happened.' She led her mother firmly towards the kitchen, but when that room turned out to be in a state of unprecedented disorder she reversed tracks to the front room, where there had been scope for serious searching, and sat the older woman down in one of the much-prized leather armchairs. 'Now,' she said.

Mrs Allbright made a visible effort, pulled herself together and spoke with more careful diction. 'I was away at the kirk and your dad was out in the fields. But he came back to the house to fetch something he'd forgotten.' She rubbed her face. 'Whether it was his knife or his pipe or his pouch or the key to the barn I dinna ken. He did tell me

156

but I misremember—'

Jill kept her patience. 'Mother,' she said. 'What happened?'

'Aren't I just telling you? Your dad came back to the house for something and walked in on them. Och, if he'd only had the sense to see that he'd everything with him!'

'Walked ... in ... on ... who, Mother?'

'Twa men,' said Mrs Allbright, coming to the point at last. 'They were ransacking the place.' She blew her nose. 'Your dad's not as young as he was or he'd have gi'en them laldie.'

'My God!' said Jill. 'Is he all right?'

'He's not as all right as he was this morning, but the doctor's been and there's nothing broken.'

'He's not in hospital, then?'

Mrs Allbright lapsed again into the Doric. 'He widna ging. He's upby the noo, in his bed, but contermit that he'll be back at work first thing.'

'I'll go and see him,' Jill said. She went out first to ensure that her car was locked up, while removing her laptop and box of disks from under the floor at the back.

She found her father, dressed in his best pyjamas, sitting up in bed and scowling at the portable television, which was showing a quiz. 'Put that damn thing off for me,' he said. 'Your mother didn't think to bring up the remote.' A bandage round his head gave him a slightly piratical air. His visible bruises were no worse than she had seen on occasions when he had had a minor accident around the farm.

'You lie down. How bad is what I can't see?' she asked.

He sank back against the pillows. 'Nothing much. Bruises and scrapes and a lump on my head like half a tennis ball, so the quack said. He put a couple of stitches in it. I'll be about in no time.'

'Maybe,' Jill said doubtfully. 'But you'll wait until the doctor says you can. Are there any jobs which can't wait?'

She waited while her father did a mental review of the farm. 'Not really,' he said at last. 'Just keeping the beasts fed.'

'I can do that. Mother can help when she gets over the shock. Tell me what happened.'

'Aye. It was this way. Your mam was away at the kirk. I wanted the shed key so I came back to the house. I was on the tractor, which must have told them I was coming. I was hardly in at the door before I got a whack on the head that put me down. I took a couple of kicks for luck. I was out for a while and when I came round they were gone and your mam was phoning for ambulances and police and Dr Swann and everybody but the SAS.'

'It's just as well that she wasn't here,' Jill remarked. 'Did you get a look at them?'

'Aye, I did. The first whack didn't put me out. It was only a glimpse, mind, but they were big lads. All I could tell the police was that one of them had a shaved head and the other had a woollen hat and hairy eyebrows. They had on jeans and something dark. That's all.'

Jill thought about it. 'What about their feet? If you were down and they kicked you, you must have seen their feet.'

He sat up again. 'You're right, by God! They both had those light-coloured safety boots that the oil companies hand out.'

'They did, did they? I'll pass that titbit on to the fuzz,' Jill said. 'What about the woollen cap. Was it in football colours?'

'You're right again. By God, I'm not surprised if yon oil company thinks the sun shines out of you. It was red and white, the colours the Dons supporters wear. I've seen it so often that I've stopped seeing it, if you ken what I mean.'

'You stay in bed for the rest of the day,' Jill said, 'or Mother will have a fit. I'll help her to get the place straightened out.'

Her father sighed. 'A proper little bossy-boots you've turned into since Oltech decided they couldn't do without you. You and Maggie Thatcher.' He looked at the

159

bedside alarm clock and then at the television. 'See if the news has started on that
damn thing, will you?'

Jill found him a news programme and
then went to phone the police.

Nothing had been stolen but the contents of
the house had been turned over and
mauled. Jill's own room looked as if a party
of drunken furniture removers had been
playing hopscotch in it. Mrs Allbright, once
she had got over the shock, seemed faintly
insulted that the intruders had ignored
some of her treasured wedding presents. Jill
soon tired of the endless speculation about
what they could possibly have wanted if not
her precious china and silver and was glad
to get back to the office on the Monday
morning.

Geoff Dubois had made good use of the
weekend and gained unrestricted and un-
supervised access to the company computer. When he visited Jill's room to say
farewell, he told her that he had as much
information as was to be gathered locally
and quite enough to begin trawling the
world of electronic banking.

'How long will it take you?' Jill asked.

'Impossible to say. Sometimes any given
piece of information may leap out at you
and sometimes you have to try all ways,

maybe write a special program and leave the machine to do its own search. All depends. I have your mobile number. We'll stay in touch.'

On a floppy disk, Jill had already established a list of staff and other associates and was feeding in her own coded symbols to demark those who would have been aware of such factors as the kitchen fire on Caber Beta and the probable effect of the strike at the company depot. Scanning the results afresh, she was discouraged. No pattern had begun to emerge, and it was uncomfortably obvious that, because anybody could have told anybody else anything at all, any pattern that did emerge would be so circumstantial as to be useless. Until more facts emerged, she would have to pin her faith on Geoff Dubois.

Any intelligent six-year-old, she told herself, could have arrived at that conclusion in a matter of seconds, but the working day had passed away unnoticed and when, after a few friendly words with her former colleagues, she emerged from the main door, her car stood in solitary state nearby. There was one other car in the far corner of the car park, an Astra about five years old. She wondered which of her friends the cleaners had scored on the Lottery or borrowed a husband's car.

161

Movement, seen in the corner of her eye. A man must have been standing close to the wall of the building, half hidden by a large berberis. He was closing in on her. Alerted by the memory of the disturbance at home, she jumped away from him, almost into the arms of another man coming from the other side. He made a grab at her computer but she jerked away. Spurred by rising panic, she took to her heels. The sudden movement caught the men by surprise. Though not wearing the most suitable of shoes, she was comparatively fleet of foot while, to judge from the pounding of feet behind her, neither man was a sprinter. She had a few yards' lead when she neared her car. Her laptop computer was in one hand but the small box of disks was safely in her coat pocket and, thankfully, she had the car key in her other hand. The remote locking was a magic wand. The locks had clicked up before her hand reached the handle.

She threw the computer, as gently as she dared, on to the passenger seat, dumped herself inside, slammed the door and slapped down the button to lock all doors.

She was just in time. One man was already at the passenger's side, wrestling with the handle. She had left the window on that side a few inches down to prevent the car's interior heating up in the spring sunshine.

The man tried to force his arm in, to reach and unlock the door. She felt for the window control but the ignition was off. She stabbed at the slot and was lucky. The key went home, she twisted and the engine fired instantly. She tried the window control again and the man cried out, gruffly, as the pressure came on his wrist like an inverted guillotine.

She had to get away. Her foot had planted itself on the accelerator and the engine was racing, but she jerked the gear selector back three clicks. Her beautiful new tyres yelped in protest and the seat gave her a push that snapped her head back.

The second man had been running across in front of the car to execute a pincer movement. The car leaped at him like a charging bull. To save his legs from being broken by the front bumper, he flung himself on to the bonnet. The car's acceleration threw him against the windscreen so that his nose was flattened and his eyes were glaring into hers. She could see the shaggy eyebrows under the woollen Dons hat. He had full lips, she noticed, and crooked teeth.

He was obscuring the whole windscreen. She swerved and braked, just in time. He was thrown off, leaving a smear of blood on the windscreen but taking one of her wipers with him. That was almost the last straw.

She was tempted to go round again and chase him about a bit but she glimpsed him somersaulting into the boundary wall of the car park. Anguished noises made her aware that the first man, his wrist still jammed in the window, was being forced to gallop faster than nature had intended any man to run. She was almost out of car park again. She hauled at the wheel, tyres protesting, and jabbed at the window control. The hand vanished but in the mirror she saw a figure run full tilt into the trunk of a tree. The other figure lay still, unconscious or preferably dead, against the low wall.

Both men were incapacitated, at least for the moment, but her first instinct was to get to hell out of there before either recovered. She tried to read the number on the Astra on the way by but she only got two letters and there was no way that was she going back. There could be more men. They could be sitting in the Astra for all that she could see through the light-reflecting windscreen. She swung out of the car park, turned towards home and then, in case of pursuit, made two more turns and parked in front of a small supermarket, breathing deeply and blinking back tears. Her heart was pounding and her mouth was very dry.

The police. Of course. With shaking hands, she groped for her mobile phone. As she did so, it began to ring. This was no time for an incoming call. She fumbled.

Mr Benjamin's voice came on the line. 'Bad time,' she said shakily. 'I'll call you back.'

'This is rather urgent.'

'So is this.' Her voice seemed determined to crack. 'I've just been attacked, about two minutes ago, in the office car park. I think they were after my computer and disks.'

'Are you all right?'

'Just shaken. I don't mean physically. I just ... just...' Jill paused and pulled herself together. 'It's over now but I must call the police.'

'Steady up. What about your attackers?'

'Hurt, lying in the office car park.'

'You play rough.'

'Yes, but listen. That's why I want to call the cops quickly, before they get away. I think they're two men who attacked my father and went through our house yesterday. They may know who sent them. The police may get it out of them.'

'Leave that to me, we can fix it from here. I want you over here right away. Hold on a moment.' She heard his voice, faintly. It returned at normal volume. 'Somebody's getting the Aberdeen police on the phone right now. Call me with a description of the men as soon as you can. For now, you've just got time to catch your plane. A seat's been reserved for you. Pick up the tickets from the BA desk. Put the other thing out of your mind for now. Go!'

Jill's emergency bag was in the back of the car but it was too bulky to take as hand luggage. She had to check it through to Miami. 'The plane's going to be up to an hour late,' said the lady behind the check-in counter. 'Fog at Gatwick. Otherwise we might not have been able to get you aboard.' Jill raised her eyes to the heavens. She was out of breath and dishevelled with haste and she could have gone home for a suitable selection of clothes ... if she had had the faintest idea what would be suitable for whatever was in store for her. She might need anything from dungarees to a ball-gown.

Jill refused to let her bag be checked straight through to Miami. She had travelled enough to know that the chances of losing luggage were greatly increased by a transfer between planes. At least she had her computer in her hand and her disks in her pocket. And her mobile phone, she remembered suddenly. She retreated into a corner of the busy concourse and called Mr Benjamin again. She gave him an account of the attack and a description of her two

166

attackers, although she had little to add to what her father had told the police. Mr Benjamin was sympathetic and solicitous. She assured him that she was recovering her composure.

Her father answered her next call. 'Dad,' she said, 'are you better?'

'I'm fine.'

'No after-effects?'

'None at all.'

'Great!' That was enough chit-chat. 'I want you to do something for me. I'm at Dyce. I'm just off to America, I don't know for how long.'

'What do you want to go there for?'

'I don't exactly want, but they can't manage without me. Listen. The spare key to my car's hidden in my handkerchief drawer. Please get Mother to drive you to Dyce and collect my car from the car park. It's about opposite the main entrance, two rows back, and the car park ticket's in the glove compartment. Drive it very carefully. Get the garage to replace the missing wiper and check it for scratches. Then keep it safely at home. I'll repay whatever you spend. And,' she said firmly, 'I know exactly how many miles are on the clock and if you drive around in it I'll know and I'll set fire to your new tractor.'

'You wouldn't.'

She could hear the amusement in her father's voice. 'I might,' she said.

She headed in the general direction of Departures. In the let-down, she felt depressed and off balance. From being chilled, she felt suddenly hot. At the bar, she found Geoff Dubois nursing a glass of beer and an evening paper. 'So you followed me!' he said. 'Couldn't put my charms out of your mind?'

Jill felt a little brighter. 'What charms?' she retorted. 'I've forgotten.'

He pointed a finger and his granny-glasses flashed at her. 'Good one! But you'll recognize my many virtues, one of these days, and then we'll set the world on fire. What really brings you here?'

'I've just had a summons from Mr Benjamin. I don't know what it's about.' They compared tickets and found that they were going to be travelling companions.

'First things first,' Geoff said. 'You look stressed out. Would a brandy be a help?'

'A great help but a bad idea,' Jill said. 'I could just about go a gin and tonic with lots of ice.'

A group in full Highland regalia, one of the men carrying a set of bagpipes, was enjoying a noisy session at the bar. As soon as he had Jill's drink and another beer for himself, Geoff led her away to a quieter corner. 'Highland dancers,' he said. 'Somebody told me they're on the way to some jamboree in Canada. They'd better lay off the sauce or they won't be allowed on the plane.' He opened his newspaper. 'I see that Oltech's had an oil spill in the Gulf of Florida. Not a big one, but they're getting a bad press. The environmentalists are kicking up hell. Could that be what your visit's about?'

Jill quickly scanned the bare facts quoted. 'I don't see how it could be,' she said. 'All I know about oil spills is that they make a hell of a mess; and if they think I'm going to clean it up with my little mop and bucket, I'll have to remind them that they don't employ me as a cleaner any more.'

'Well, I don't know. They seem to think you're the fairy with the magic wand these days. If your summons is because they've found out who the traitor is, for God's sake see that somebody lets me know before I waste a lot of time and break a lot of laws.'

Their plane was called soon after that. Geoff managed to exchange seats with a fat woman so that they could sit together. After a long wait on the tarmac it took off. The meal was small and tasteless but there was wine with it. Jill ate gratefully. Geoff bought her another gin and tonic.

At Gatwick, Jill reclaimed her bag. They changed terminals. They should have missed their connection, but the day of fog had reduced the timetables to a shambles. They were given boarding passes for a flight which might or might not have been the one on which seats had originally been booked and Jill checked her bag in again. She had split a fingernail while lugging the bag around, so she dug a little manicure case out of it before checking it in for Miami.

They had time to fill. The lounge was noisy, stuffy and crowded with miserable travellers, but Geoff found her a seat near the bar and, despite her protests, bought her another drink. She was beginning to float. Focusing carefully, she began to trim her broken nail. She was tired and her head was beginning to thump.

Among the waiting travellers were the Highland dancers. There could be no doubt that they had continued with what had become a very jolly party. Cheered on by his companions, the piper suddenly inflated his bag and struck up a lively march. The noise filled the lounge and brought conversation to a halt.

One or two of the waiting throng tapped their feet but most looked as though this were the last straw and they would rather have been left in peace with their misery.

Jill's own attitude to the pipes was ambivalent. Her father had explained that the instrument had been devised so that, in time of war, a marching musician could accompany the fighting troops and play rousing music without pausing to draw breath. Fair enough. Played on one mountain-top and heard from another, it was stirring stuff. But the limited notes of the chanter accompanied by the unchanging chord of the drones did not produce the most mellifluous music and, in her weakened and slightly fuddled condition, she did not welcome the noise in a confined space and only a few feet away.

'God Almighty!' said Geoff. He had to repeat the remark more loudly and almost into her ear before she could make out what he was saying.

One of the dancers attempted a *pas de bas*, stepped on his own foot and fell down. The piper stepped back to give him room, nearly treading in his turn on Jill's foot. Her head began to ring.

The bag was now just in front of her face. Without giving herself time to think, she raised her nail scissors and snipped.

The result outreached her expectations. The piper's elbow slapped down to his side as the air and a gust of whisky fumes escaped around Jill's ears. The sound was cut off so suddenly that the raised voices in the lounge seemed like a silence. Somebody cheered.

The piper swung round. He was a fat man with a wispy moustache and he was sweating. He looked for a culprit and settled on Geoff. 'You done it,' he said thickly.

Geoff rose to his full height, topping the piper by a foot. 'I did not,' he said.

'I did it,' Jill said. She moved the scissors a few inches to a position just below the hem of the kilt. 'And if you don't bugger off, just have a guess what I'm going to snip next.'

The piper backed hurriedly away and fell over his fallen crony.

Nine

Geoff, being the taller, could only sit, contorted, and endure. Jill managed to sleep for part of the flight. She washed and tidied herself in the aircraft toilet and managed to wake up again. They reclaimed their bags from the carousel and parted company.

Jill was claimed by a lean man with sharp blue eyes and a weatherbeaten face. Her first impression was of a big man, but when she saw that he was no taller than herself she realized that she was being deluded by his air of superabundant energy. His accent, she thought, was again Texan. 'Mr Benjamin sends his apologies, ma'am,' he said. He took her arm and started walking and Jill perforce had to follow. 'John Backus. I'm to take you straight out to Largo Twelve.'

'Nobody said anything to me...'

He paused in his stride. 'You don't have working duds with you? That could be a problem.'

'I've got my gear with me. But Largo Twelve ... Isn't that where they've got a

173

problem with Greenpeace?'

He set off again through a set of automatic doors. Leaving the air-conditioned building with its washed and filtered air was like entering a sauna with overtones of dead fish and mildew. Jill made a sound and he caught her expression. 'The locals say that this is the smell of money, get used to it or get lost. No, they're not Greenpeace, ma'am, though they're giving the media that impression. Some kind of an offshoot, I guess. You can change in the back of the chopper. We won't peek.'

Jill tried without success to slow down their march. The hangars seemed to be a mile off and she dreaded the walk in such heat, but he led her to where a young man was waiting in what seemed to be an over-sized golf cart which could have held a dozen people. They found shade under its green and white striped canopy. 'But what on earth or off it am I supposed to do about it?' Jill asked as the cart moved off.

'Beats the hell out of me, ma'am. But the head honcho of the group seems to know you and says he won't trust anyone else. Seems Conimoco had a sit-in last year and promised all they were asked for and then reneged *and* prosecuted.'

'So why would he trust me?'

He grinned suddenly. 'Why not? *I'd* trust

you and I'm as suspicious as they come. You've had a good press.' Jill had given up trying to slow him down but as they neared a hangar complex on the edge of the airport, he stopped suddenly. 'Better talk here, ma'am. It'll be noisy on the chopper. I'm to tell you that the oil spill they're griping about was suspected sabotage, that we're stepping up security to see that it doesn't happen again, that we had the slick cleared before it did a damn bit of environmental damage and that we're overhauling our safety and containment procedures. Mr Benjamin says they'll be welcome to come and check over what we're doing in that respect. And that's as far as we're prepared to go. If they don't get the hell off our rig and let us start drilling again they'll be removed by force and to hell with public relations. I guess that's what they're looking for all along.'

'I see. In other words, it's one great cock-up so they dump it on me.'

'Yep. That sums it up.'

'And you reckon that what the protesters are really after is to do Oltech the maximum PR damage that they can?'

'Can't see what else they have to gain.'

'And they asked for me because they thought it would take days to get me here?'

'Seems likely.'

'They were wrong. What this head honcho's name?'

'No idea. Do they have names?'

The cart was quick and the breeze it made was welcome. The young driver brought them quickly along two rows of hangars to where the helicopter was already on the ramp. It could have carried an infantry platoon but on the outward trip the only passengers were Jill, John Backus and a drilling engineer who spent the trip engrossed in his Sony laptop carrying a technical report liberally illustrated with graphs and histograms. The pilot went through his checklist with practised ease, started the motors and lifted off.

As soon as they were airborne, the air-conditioning system introduced a blessed cool but the noise level was almost intolerable and Jill was glad of the soft foam earplugs handed out by the pilot. She kitted herself out in the comparative privacy of a rear seat, freshened herself with the aid of several sachets of moist paper cloth saved from the aircraft and then spent the trip looking down on the yachts and commercial vessels and, later, the patterns of reef and sandbank. She had gone past the need for sleep.

At last, the pilot singled out one of several widespread rigs. Jill noticed that several large inflatables were moored against one of the legs. The helicopter settled with hardly a bump on the helipad. Several men and a woman, each wearing hard hats with the company logo and carrying a luggage bag, were waiting for transport back to shore and the three passengers had hardly reached the bottom of the first metal stair before the helicopter was embarking them.

The pilot had come to the doorway. 'No need to hurry yourselves,' he said. 'My orders are to wait awhile and see if I don't have some of that rentamob to take back with me.' Jill nodded. That explained the size of the helicopter, which she had put down at first to typical American overkill.

There was a brisk breeze. Hastily, Jill donned her hard hat. She and John Backus were met by a small delegation led by the OIM, who introduced himself as Grant Abrahams. 'Glad you're here, Miss All-bright,' he said. 'They may talk to you but they'll only shout at anyone else. Go careful. There are reporters there, trying to melt in among them.'

Jill shook his hand but her mind was leaping ahead. 'Why do you think the leak was sabotage?' she asked.

Mr Abrahams was an exception to the general run of oil-men, being slim and delicate-looking, but he was quick and businesslike. 'There is no way that those bolts could have slacked themselves off. Let's go. Get rid of the bastards and let us get on with drilling. Company orders are to do nothing to provoke a confrontation, at least until you've had your ten cents' worth, but it's as much as I can do to keep our roughnecks from giving them an accidental dose of the water-and-oil mixture.'

He led them, clattering, through the functional complexity of the rig. From a gallery above the separators, men were looking down impassively to where, beneath the derrick, a dozen or more people, mostly young and mostly scruffily dressed, were lounging around the wellhead. Backpacks and rolled sleeping-bags had been stowed among the machinery. The deck was littered with bags and papers and emptied plastic bottles. There was a stirring as Jill appeared. At first glance she could not pick out the reporters, but there was no hiding the large video-camera. Two other men, slightly older than the average, seemed to be keeping their hands out of sight and she guessed that they were holding cameras.

She put down her bag. 'Who's the big cheese here?' she asked loudly.

A tubby young man with ginger hair turned and stepped forward. 'I don't recognize the description, but I suppose I am,' he said. 'Hello, Jill.'

The square, freckled face was familiar but hard to place. She tried fitting him against a variety of backgrounds. When she had worked back to her teens, the penny dropped. 'Well, well, well. Bill Boddam.'

He nodded, smiling at an old friend. 'You've been living an exciting life since we were neighbours.'

One of the men was holding a microphone almost under her nose, yet trying to be surreptitious about it. Jill felt sudden relief. This might not be so difficult after all. In a hasty mental review of the situation, she decided that friendship would only weaken her position and so was not the line to pursue. 'We'll meet for a chat about old times later,' she said coldly. 'First, get your friends off the rig so that we can resume our proper and legal business.'

He smiled more broadly, enjoying his taste of power. 'Not so fast. We'll go, but there are certain conditions.'

'What conditions?'

'We want a clean-up operation and compensation for damage to the environment.'

'The clean-up was completed some time ago,' Jill said loudly, for the benefit of the microphone and whole party. 'If we missed anything, tell us and we'll deal with it. As far as I'm aware there was no environmental damage but, if there had been, who would you have suggested we compensate? You personally?'

She was pleased to note that he still flushed rather easily. 'You don't have to throw suggestions like that around. A contribution to the World Wildlife Fund might do it,' he said. 'And we want some guarantees that it won't happen again.'

'It won't happen again,' Jill said firmly. 'We're tightening security to prevent the same sort of malicious damage being repeated. We're checking and revising our safety and containment procedures and I'm to tell you that you're welcome to come and check what we do in that respect and bring your reporter friends with you.'

'We want guarantees,' he said stubbornly.

'And just what guarantees do you have in mind?'

Thinking had evidently not proceeded so far ahead. He shrugged.

Jill had had time to think. Meanwhile the visitors had closed in, crowding around. Little was said, but they were exuding hostility. Two reporters were pushing microphones almost into her face. Jill felt claustrophobic. Moreover, what she had to say was not for the public ear. 'Move back, all of you,' she said. 'Let us have a word in reasonable privacy.'

Bill Boddam produced a sneer. 'If you want to offer me a bribe, I can tell you now that it won't be accepted.'

'You should be so lucky,' Jill said. She leaned forward and whispered two or three words in his ear. They took a few moments to register. Then he paled suddenly and his face took on a pinched look. When he had recovered, he said, stiff-lipped, 'Move back everybody. I'll hear what the lady has to say.'

One of the reporters objected but Boddam turned and shouted at him to back off. The crush pulled back. Jill drew him in the other direction. The watching throng saw only that they were whispering together. Boddam suddenly raised his voice. 'I don't believe that this is happening,' he said.

'You'd better bloody well believe it,' Jill retorted grimly. 'You fetched me all the way from the north of Scotland because you said that I was the one person you could believe. So believe me.'

They spoke again in whispers. Boddam gesticulated, Jill made calming gestures. Suddenly Boddam turned away. His face had gone from white to scarlet. 'Gather up your things,' he said hoarsely. 'We've got all we came for.'

There was a chorus of protest and questions but he kept shaking his head.

'The helicopter is waiting for anyone who

wants a ride back to shore,' Jill said. 'The rest can take the inflatables. Or swim for all I care. Mr Boddam is staying –' she looked at her watch, could it really still be so early? '– staying for a second breakfast, which is all the bribe that he's going to get out of it, in case anyone's wondering. I'm ready now to talk to him about old times.'

There was confusion and even disbelief, but Jill and Boddam were both adamant.

A Cadillac with a uniformed driver collected Jill from the heliport and set her down gently under the porte-cochère of a tall glass building on the outskirts of downtown Miami. Large birds, which the driver said were turkey vultures, circled high overhead. It was early afternoon and the heat and humidity were oppressive. Inside the automatic doors, however, air-conditioning produced an atmosphere which dried the sweat on her back in seconds. A dozen people were passing through the lobby or talking with the two behind the reception desk. None of their faces was familiar but most of them paused to give her a smile or a small gesture of salutation. Word, it seemed, had gone ahead of her.

A secretary was waiting for her in the lobby – a middle-aged lady with a restrained figure and sculpted hair in a dress which was almost a clone of her own. Jill wondered whether Mr Benjamin's taste had figured in the choice of both. She had changed back into her office dress, but the secretary's perfect make-up and deportment reminded her that rather a long time had passed since she had enjoyed a bath and a change to clean clothing. She was whisked upwards in a silent lift. As it halted and the doors sighed open, she said, 'I want a few minutes in the ladies' room ... toilet ... bathroom ... whatever you call it over here. Rest room, isn't it?'

'Mr Benjamin wished to see you the very minute you arrived. Please come this way.'

'Is this the way to the rest room?'

'Mr Benjamin is waiting.'

Jill was tired and sticky and had the beginning of another headache. 'I get a few minutes in the rest room or Mr Benjamin doesn't get to see me at all.' The woman's meticulous English added to her scandalized expression were clue enough. 'Didn't I speak to you on the phone one night?'

'You did,' the secretary said tersely.

'Then you must know how determined I can get. Let's not waste any more of Mr Benjamin's time than we have to.'

The secretary was not going to demean herself by escorting Jill to the toilet. She pointed loftily. 'The rest rooms are along there. Second door on the left.'

Jill, still carrying her bag, found her way. An anxious examination in a huge mirror told her that she looked as secondhand and dog-eared as she felt, but that might have been partly due to the cruel lighting. She enjoyed a thorough wash with a better soap than had been available on Largo Twelve, brushed her hair and renewed her very slight make-up. She still felt slightly shop-soiled but she thought that she might pass muster at a slight distance.

The secretary was waiting, showing signs of exaggerated patience. Jill walked slowly for the pleasure of seeing her seethe.

Benjamin Hochmeinster was seated behind a large and scrupulously tidy desk in a cool, bright room overlooking a waterway where an expensive-looking ketch was heading in the direction which she thought was seaward. He jumped up and came round the desk to shake her hand. He was as smooth and well presented as ever. A large smile, the first that she had ever seen him produce, sat well on his bulldog face. 'First things first,' he said. 'Are you hungry?'

'I seem to have been eating irregularly and piecemeal for days,' Jill said. 'You know how it is. But I can last a little longer.'

'Coffee, then?'

Jill found that the air-conditioning had

already dried her mouth. 'Coffee would be great.'

Mr Benjamin nodded to the secretary and led Jill to a group of comfortable chairs. The secretary left with what was recognizably a flounce. 'I want you to stay over,' he said. 'Get to know something of the set-up. I'd invite you to visit with me except that I live alone and the office staff get ideas only too easily, so you're booked into the Rougemont Plaza Hotel. I know you left home in a hurry, so I'll have somebody take you to the shops at Bayview and then to the hotel and I'll pick you up at eight for dinner, if that suits?'

Slightly stunned, Jill said that it would suit very well.

'That's fine. Now, tell me what inducements you used to get them off the rig. We'll honour any undertaking you gave, if it's within our powers.'

Jill fought back a yawn. The secretary was pouring coffee. 'I didn't offer him any sexual favours, if that's what you mean,' Jill said. She heard the secretary catch her breath and the coffee pot clinked against a cup. 'I blackmailed him instead,' Jill continued. Coffee slopped into a saucer. The secretary went out to fetch a clean cup and saucer.

'Well,' Mr Benjamin said, 'you've shocked the hell out of Miss Morgan, which is exactly what you intended, and God knows she needs it at times. So now you can tell me for real.'

'That was for real.' Jill waited while Miss Morgan returned, rigid with disapproval, and finished her ministrations. 'We used to live almost next door,' Jill resumed. 'He asked for me because he thought that he could trust me. Or possibly because he thought it would take me an age to get there. But I happened to remember an incident from years ago, a ridiculous and disgraceful event that he didn't know I knew about. It was exactly the sort of thing he'd least want the world to be giggling over. I threatened to go on a chat show with it or to give it to your PR people to spread around and do what they liked with. After it sank in, I could have made him do a streak though the White House.'

Mr Benjamin's eyes were alight with amusement. 'And what was this disgraceful incident?' he asked.

Jill shook her head. 'I promised that I wouldn't repeat it. And I was only there because he trusted me. Just take my word for it, you won't have any more trouble with him.'

Mr Benjamin regarded her with amusement. 'I'll get it out of you before we're much older.'

'Don't hold your breath.'

'I had no such intention.' They were talking like old friends. He sighed. 'Well, that's a very satisfactory conclusion.'

Jill fought back another yawn. 'Not quite a conclusion, not yet. The whole episode was part of a sustained campaign to get the company a bad name. Bill Boddam got a substantial back-hander and more money to spread around, to organize as much adverse publicity as he could squeeze out of it. I took him to breakfast on the rig and shook the story out of him. The coffee's very good out there, by the way, but the eggs were too hard.'

There was no longer any sign of amusement on Mr Benjamin's pug-face. 'That's pretty much what we suspected. No, I don't mean the eggs, as you very well know.'

'I haven't quite finished yet. He overheard something which suggested that there's a major act of sabotage planned. He didn't know what or where.'

By now, Mr Benjamin's eyes were looking past her and through the far wall. His face was grim. 'I'll see that a warning goes out to all our establishments and ships,' he said at last. 'And the company may have even more cause to be grateful to you. So who's behind it?'

'He didn't know. The most he could give

me was a description of the man who approached him.'

'Tell me.' Mr Benjamin picked up a pencil and pad.

Jill closed her eyes in the effort of recall. 'Medium height but very heavily built. Aged about fifty. Small ears, slightly protruding. Thin lips. Large nose with broken veins. High colour. Black hair receding and thinning on top. Dark bags under his eyes. Upper teeth rather crooked in front. Oh yes, and a tenor voice with an accent that Bill put down as London. I think that's all.'

'That's a good description. We'll send out some faxes and see who recognizes it.' He sat back in his chair and toyed with his cup and saucer. 'There's a story circulating around the office ... Is it true that you slashed a piper's bag at the airport and then threatened to neuter him?'

Jill frowned. Perhaps the smiles which had greeted her in the lobby had not all been of congratulation. 'And to think that Geoff Dubois told me that he was good at keeping secrets!' she said.

'But is it true?'

'Quite true. The man was deafening me.'

The laughter came back to his eyes. 'I must remind staff to lower their voices when you're around.'

As Jill left the room he was on the office phone, calling Miss Morgan to come and take dictation. A driver was waiting in the lobby to take her to the shops.

Ten

The next few days went by in a haze of activity.

Mr Benjamin took Jill to dinner on that first evening. Jill had shopped carefully, bathed and slept, so that she was cool and refreshed as well as being merely clean. Mr Benjamin, when he called for her, was his usual formal, courteous self, but Jill sensed that he had become more aware of her as a person – not as a physical, female presence but as a colleague who had the knack or the luck to pull corporate irons out of fires. He had also relaxed enough to laugh at her jokes and, between extracting detailed reports on her researches to date, her encounter in the car park and her clash of wills on Largo Twelve, he demanded and chuckled over the full story of the piper and his bag. At the close of the evening, he went so far as to administer a warm handshake in the hotel lobby, retaining his clasp for a little longer than demanded by convention. Jill thought that, given a little encouragement, he might even have kissed her fingertips. From the depths of her inexperience she supposed that such a chaste and platonic relationship must be almost unique in the world of business, but she could well imagine that he found it necessary to be very circumspect in his relationships. Any attempt at flirtation might well be construed as harassment.

Thereafter, she hardly saw him for several days. She had a brief and satisfactory interview, in an enormous office which seemed to have been furnished with cleverly recycled driftwood, with Mr Hochmeinster Senior (who in his turn insisted on being regaled with the story of the bagpiper). Mr Hochmeinster was much less intimidating in person than his photograph had led her to expect. He seemed to look on her as he might a favourite niece. Jill suspected that he was relieved and delighted to have one of his sudden hunches hit the jackpot. Using the minimum of words, he managed to milk her of every detail of her activities on behalf of the company. Jill was impressed but not overawed.

She was then passed from hand to hand and taken on whirlwind tours of offices, depots, a refinery, a group of onshore wells and the subsidiaries of Oltech that shared in the headquarters building. Her hotel catered mainly for transient trade and although there was good room service the restaurant only opened for breakfast, but a succession of presentable young men had been delegated to fill her evenings. Jill sucked in information with all the patience and concentration that she could muster and enjoyed the company of her escorts without yielding to the several attempts on her virtue. Presumably someone would tell her when it was time to go home. She was in no hurry.

On the Friday afternoon, the still disapproving Miss Morgan collected her from the design office of the pipework subsidiary and delivered her to Mr Benjamin along with the customary supply of excellent coffee. When Jill arrived, he was on the phone and dealing out clear, calm instructions about a minor dispute with a fuel retailer, but he smiled with his eyes and pointed to a chair. At his nod, Miss Morgan poured coffee and departed. Jill decided that, whether she knew it or not, Miss Morgan was nursing unrequited love for Mr Benjamin and possibly for his father as well. After several minutes, the call finished.

In answer to his enquiries, she was able to assure him that she had enjoyed her visit and now had a better idea of the workings of the company. When he was satisfied, he got down to business. 'First, I owe it to you to bring you up to date. We took the information you ... extracted from your childhood buddy very seriously. We warned all our staff and contractors to be very much on their guards. We know that at least one attempted sabotage was averted. The skipper of one of our largest tankers had had his suspicions of his third officer, who had been seen talking to some shady characters and seemed to have more money than he should. The skipper arranged for him to be watched closely and he was seen to have planted some sort of device. The ship was to have caught fire in the English Channel, right where it would have cost us the most money, caused the most disruption to shipping and done the worst possible environmental damage. The effect on public relations would have been disastrous and would certainly have had an effect on the official attitude to our tenders for future licences.'

'That would be the Scottish Office?' Jill asked.

'No. The Department of Trade and Industry in Whitehall, the same body that is responsible for matters of environmental pollution. So it seems, Miss Allbright, that you are continuing to be our lucky talisman.'

Jill murmured something deprecatory

while inwardly glowing. She had never been called a talisman before.

'We have learned the identity,' Mr Benjamin resumed, 'of the man who approached your friend Bill Boddam. Unfortunately, he is not an regular employee of any company but a freelance, and we haven't yet found out who he was representing. A direct approach might do more harm than good, so we are having him investigated and watched.

'So much for what has gone by. To look to the future, there will be a meeting on Monday with our suppliers and subsidiaries, to finalize our bids for the next round of licence areas on the European continental shelf. Highly confidential though that meeting will be, I would like you to enlarge your understanding of what's at stake by staying on and attending the meeting – just as an observer, you understand?'

Jill nodded. 'Won't the Aberdeen City Police be getting impatient to interview me about the attack?'

'I expect so. They have been told that you'll make a statement as soon as you're back in Britain. They have your descriptions, but until they make an identification there's not much more that you could contribute.'

That seemed almost logical but, after a

moment's thought, Jill's intuition took over. She pointed an accusing finger at him. 'You're hoping that your own men in Aberdeen can find them first. What have you tried? Private detectives? Bribing the police?'

Mr Benjamin looked shocked. 'The question doesn't arise because they seem to have dropped out of sight. Why would I think along those lines?'

'Because your agents could shake more information out of them than the police would ever be allowed to. It's all right,' she added comfortingly. 'I'm not shocked. They deserve it. They damaged my new car. Among other things,' she added quickly.

'You'll stay, then? You would be welcome to fly home for the weekend at the company's expense.'

Jill was beginning to acclimatize and the prospect of two long and two short air trips, separated by only a few hours at home, a no doubt fractious interview with the police and two shifts of the clock, even with a possible date with David Banion in mind, had little attraction for her. 'I'll stay over,' she said. 'I can do some sightseeing or get a tan.'

'I think you're very sensible. Flying is a squalid way to travel and one should do the absolute minimum of it. How would you occupy yourself for the weekend? Have you made any friends in Miami?'

'None that I could dump myself on for the weekend.'

'That's a pity. I would have entertained you myself, but I have to fly to California this evening for the wedding of a favourite niece and I shan't be back before Sunday evening. However, I have a suggestion to make. I've agreed to lend my boat to my cousin, Ed Marsh. He's a non-executive director, by the way. He has his own diving company and we use his services now and again. Anyway, I'm lending him my boat to make up a party tomorrow, yourself included, for a trip, maybe to the Keys or to Bimini and back. You could get your tan on board. Would that suit you?'

'It sounds great,' Jill said. It certainly sounded better than idling around Miami with little or no local knowledge. The father of a friend had kept a sloop in Stonehaven harbour and she had sailed to Norway and back several times.

'I'll tell Ed. Then, on Sunday, is there anywhere particular you'd like to go?'

'I've been hearing a lot about the Everglades,' Jill said. 'Do they run conducted tours?'

'They surely do. A wind-boat with two big fans takes you in and out of the channels and lagoons, shows you alligators and whatever. I'll have somebody arrange it and a car will pick you up.'

Despite the unaccustomed warmth and humidity, Jill had formed the habit of walking between the office building and her hotel for the sake of the exercise. As she crossed the foyer on her way out, Geoff Dubois's gangling figure was approaching. He did a U-turn to walk with her, talking vaguely about the weather.

When they were outside, he said softly, 'I wanted to give you a report and you've got me believing that there are ears everywhere.'

'This seems pretty secure,' Jill said. 'Americans don't walk. They either go jogging or they motor everywhere. How are you getting on?'

'I've gone almost as far as I can go. You won't find it as helpful as you hoped. Most accounts have irregular deposits. Mostly small but they can add up. Some of those are people I know play the horses or visit casinos. Ten to twenty have made large deposits – depending on what you consider large. I've managed to eliminate around half because I could trace the payment to a bookie. Or to a realtor, which suggests that it's for the sale of property. I've no easy way of checking on that.'

'That would be a nice, safe channel for a

bribe,' Jill said. 'What about secret accounts in different names?'

'This may surprise you. Seven of the top names have secret bank accounts under different names. But mostly those accounts have been set up using an open transfer from a main account. Sometimes that could be for tax reasons or to keep money out of the hands of an ex-wife.'

They waited at a street crossing for the lights to change. Another pedestrian, a Hispanic type, was waiting. When they were across and out of earshot of the other, Jill said, 'What you've got so far, is it on disk?'

'I can transfer it to disk.'

'Do that, please. And let's not meet again for a while. Put the disk in an envelope and give it to the manager at my hotel, to go in the safe with my computer and my own disks. That's where I deposit them overnight.'

'Will do. You don't trust anybody, do you?'

'Up to a fortnight ago, I trusted everybody. Now I'm learning better. There seem to be hostile forces around.'

'Do you trust me?'

The question surprised Jill. 'I suppose so,' she said. 'Why would you care?'

'I was hoping you trusted me enough to invite me up to your room for a friendly drink.'

Jill laughed. 'That much I do not trust any man. You can buy me a drink at the bar, if you insist.'

'I do. I look on it as bread upon the waters. Not that I'm religious, you understand.'

'I'd gathered that,' Jill said.

After her usual light breakfast, Jill left word with the reception desk and went out on to the terrace beside the small swimming-pool. After the air-conditioned interior, the heat and humidity were already oppressive but there was a light breeze coming in from seaward and the smell of salt water brought back good memories. The weekend traffic of yachts and small fishing vessels was riffling the calm of the waterway below the terrace and she looked forward to escaping to sea with them.

Ed Marsh, Mr Benjamin's cousin, found her leaning on the balustrade and thinking, for once, about nothing in particular. They shook hands. He was a remarkably hairy man even to the nose and ears and, although he seemed to have shaved with care, his chin was already blue. He was strongly built. Jill guessed his age to be in the early forties but his face was so strongly modelled that the movement of its every jaw muscle seemed to be exaggerated. All in all, Jill felt that he was a little too macho to be true, and this seemed to be borne out by a patronizing manner and the presence at the door of an open Porsche, scarlet with a white interior. He spoke little, concentrating on carving a contemptuous path through the other traffic.

Twenty minutes brought them to a yacht basin where Jill estimated that the value of the assembled yachts would have exceeded the gross annual product of a small republic. Tall masts nodded, reflecting the sun, and big motor-cruisers sat hunched on the water. A steady foot-traffic of people in colourful leisurewear was ferrying stores along the boardwalks to the yachts. He parked the Porsche carefully in the shade beside the dockmaster's office, nodded to the man in the doorway and they set off along a boardwalk. It was cooler so near the water.

'Have you sailed before?' Ed Marsh asked.

'A little.'

'Could be useful.' He looked up at the sky. 'Not that we're likely to get a breeze for sailing. But there's a good motor. You have a swimsuit?'

'I'm wearing it under this dress,' Jill said.

Mr Benjamin's yacht, *Laughing Girl*, lay at the far end of the boardwalk and near to the main channel. Jill was impressed. *Laughing Girl* was a sloop of about forty feet overall, comfortably beamy and absolutely immaculate. Varnish, paintwork and stainless steel all gleamed while the sails were neatly furled and covered and the halliards were frapped to prevent them rapping against the mast. The yacht, Jill decided, was the possession of either a proud or a fussy owner and yet, in its present company, comparatively modest.

At the gangway, they met a man in shorts, singlet and a peaked cap, carrying a varnish brush. He glanced at Jill before touching the peak of the cap to Ed Marsh. 'Mr Hochmeinster phoned to say that you'd be taking her out. She's all ready, Mr Marsh, and she's fuelled up.'

'Thanks, Joe.' A bill changed hands.

They gained the deck. There was an awning for shade over the cockpit. Marsh opened the companionway down to the main cabin. 'You can get rid of the dress down there,' he said. 'There's sun-block in a bottle on the shelf. Better use it. If you've sailed before, I guess you know that you get a double dose of sun on the water. I can do your back for you.'

Descending four steps into a trim and homely cabin, Jill decided that Ed Marsh's manner was becoming just a little too proprietary. She would apply the sun-cream for herself and if that meant that she had to

201

keep her shoulderblades away from the sun, so be it. She had bought a smart and not too immodest bikini. She kept her sandals on. She was applying the lotion when she heard and felt the engine start. The mutter changed its note and the slanting sunlight began to move across the cabin sole. She finished up quickly and made her way back into the cockpit.

Ed Marsh had removed his shirt, revealing a torso with a pelt which Jill could only think would resemble that of a grizzly bear. He was at the wheel and they were under way. Already the dock was receding into the middle distance. There was nobody else to be seen.

'Where are the others?' she asked.

He seemed genuinely surprised. 'What others?'

'Mr Benjamin said that you'd be taking out a party.'

He shrugged his hairy shoulders. 'He didn't say that to me, just asked me to give you a day out. I guess you're the party.'

Jill was unsure whether to be alarmed or relieved. The prospect of a day spent making conversation with strangers from backgrounds vastly different from her own had been perturbing her. On the other hand, time spent on the water with a hairy stranger who was exuding pheromones by the litre was equally unsettling. The distance to shore was already rather far to swim, she would only create a scene and ill-will if she demanded a U-turn and if Mr Benjamin had arranged the trip it must surely be all right, but she would have felt more comfortable if she had had her mobile phone with her. In the confines of the cockpit and beneath the awning, she felt herself cramped too close to his oppressive presence. She stepped up on to the side-deck and walked forward to the very bow. The sun was strong but the breeze from their motion softened it. She faced the sunshine, closed her eyes and put her head back. At least she would be able to go home with a tan.

Time passed. She fell into a reverie, lulled by the gentle rise and fall, mulling over the extraordinary change that had come over her life in so short a time and trying to make sense of the many small hints which had been offering themselves, sometimes half-recognized, to her consciousness.

After a while the vibration of the engine, which she had felt through her feet, died away and the splutter of the exhaust was silenced. *Laughing Girl* slowed, came to a halt and turned slowly to adjust to a slight seaway coming in from the south-east. The pitching changed to a gentle roll.

Ed Marsh was moving around in the cockpit. His head appeared over the coach-roof. 'I'm ready for a swim,' he called. 'Coming in?' Without waiting for an answer, he dived over the side, entering cleanly with hardly a splash.

Jill felt warm and sticky and she would very much have liked to swim in the green water, but the water was very clear and it was only too obvious that he had not felt obliged to wear trunks. The conventions might be different, here in Florida, but swimming with a naked man, a far from perfect stranger, was not part of her agenda. Even his buttocks, she noticed, were hairy. We come from monkeys, she told herself, but some have not come very far. On the other hand, monkeys' bottoms, she seemed to remember, were relatively hairless. Perhaps evolution was now moving in some contrary direction. Such skin as showed was deeply tanned.

He swam underwater towards the bow before surfacing and shaking water from his head. 'Are you coming?' he repeated.

'I can't swim,' Jill said firmly.

'No point inviting you for a skinny-dip, then. It's your loss. The water's great.'

He took off in a powerful crawl. Jill thought that he was showing off in the hope of impressing her. He surged away, circled

204

the yacht and then climbed aboard over the stern. He began to dry himself in the cockpit. So, she thought, he must have some sense of decency left. 'There are drinks below,' he called. 'Are you coming?'

Jill looked around but the only vessels to be seen were on the horizon. Some of the yachts had their sails set but they were making little progress. Mr Benjamin or no Mr Benjamin, she had no intention of entering the cabin along with a naked stranger. 'I rather like it here,' she retorted. 'I don't see a lot of the sun where I come from.'

'OK.'

He disappeared below. She hoped that he would have donned at least a pair of trunks before he surfaced again. Or perhaps he counted his nakedness as covered by his shaggy pelt. If so, he was seriously mistaken.

After several minutes he reappeared and came forward. He was carrying a tray with two glasses, an insulated jug and the bottle of sunblock. She was relieved to note that he was wearing the towel around his waist. He held out the tray. 'Daiquiris,' he said. His voice had thickened and, meeting his eye for a moment, Jill thought that the glass he selected for himself was not his first drink. This was going to demand care. She accepted the other but took only a sip. It was very strong. She had been plied with daiquiris in the past. On this as on other occasions, she preferred to keep her inhibitions intact.

'Is my cousin Ben sleeping with you?' he asked suddenly.

'Definitely not. He's been a perfect gentleman.' A dissociated corner of her mind decided that his question would have been less blatantly chauvinist if the phrasing had been reversed.

He nodded as if reassured. His closeness implied an unwanted intimacy. She retreated as far as she could, but the stainless steel of the pulpit rail had heated under the sun and she felt it burning against the back of her thighs. He saw her flinch. With what was intended as a courtly gesture, he whipped off the towel one-handed and held it out to her. Jill's impulse was to hold it up in front of her as a protection from his probing eyes but the sun was reflecting off the water as well as burning down. Her upper back was beginning to prickle ominously and if she stepped away from the pulpit rail she would have to approach almost into his grasp. She threw the towel over her shoulders. It was damp and long enough to give her protection from the hot metal. She muttered a gruff thankyou.

Ed Marsh, meantime, had finished his drink. He looked around vaguely. The yacht's coach-roof ended only a few feet behind him and the fore hatch was near the forward edge. He took a pace backward and seated himself on the hatch, putting the tray down at his feet. His hands freed, he poured himself another drink. Jill could have shot most of hers over the side while his attention was elsewhere but he would only have offered her another and, if he was going to turn amorous, she felt more able to cope with a fuddled pursuer than a sober one. She sipped. And at least, she thought, on a low seat and with his knees together, his nakedness was not so flaunted.

'So Ben's being his usual prissy self?' he said thickly. 'Thinks too much of himself to be human. I'm not like that.'

He waited.

'You're not?' Jill ventured.

He shook his head emphatically. 'I'm the manly type. Self-made. Ben would be nothing if it wasn't for the old man's bucks. Me, what I have I've earned.' He laughed sharply. 'I'll tell you something else. A girl told me once that I have a very affectionate nature. And it's true, I'm one of nature's lovers.' He studied her. 'You're very beautiful,' he said at last. 'Your figure is ... exquisite. Too good to spoil by getting white marks all over it. Why don't you take off that bikini and get an all-over tan?'

'I'm happy as I am, thank you,' Jill said. There was no longer any doubt about his intentions. To yield to his approaches would be the simplest way out of any confrontation and would be the route which many girls would have taken. But, although she had no rooted objection to sex in principle, her previous experience had been little and less than satisfying. Sex with a hirsute stranger of unknown medical history was just not on. She had a mad thought that, if he invited her to run her fingers through his hair, she would not know where to begin...

Perhaps he was all mouth and no action. But no. His eyes were losing focus but there was still a grim and determined look about them. She was definitely in a trap. She could not get past him without coming within reach of a grab. It seemed that mention of Mr Benjamin's name was not an effective turn-off. Perhaps, she thought, she could get past him by feinting to one side and then running along the other side-deck to the cockpit where there were winch handles and a boathook to use as weapons.

He seemed to be in no hurry but to be enjoying himself eyeing her and playing on his intimidation of her. Perhaps if she span out the talk he would drink himself into impotence.

'You have a boyfriend?' he asked.

On the point of admitting that her present relationship was unconsummated, Jill changed her mind. 'I'm going steady with a champion wrestler,' she said. 'He's very jealous.'

The champion wrestler was dismissed with a gesture which spilled daiquiri on to Mr Benjamin's immaculate teak decking. It dried within seconds. Ed Marsh screwed his face into an expression of affability. 'He's a very lucky man. You were made for loving. But I won't tell him if you don't and he needn't get his balls in an uproar over anything he doesn't know about. The minute I saw you, I thought, "That lady could make a man very, very happy." And it's true. Did you ever think about the temptation you offer, going around looking like a centrefold? Hey?'

Jill decided against denying that she looked like a centrefold. That was a subject which might have led almost anywhere. She kept fear out of her voice. 'Flattery will get you nowhere.'

Ed Marsh seemed to find the information disappointing. ' 'Snot flattery. You're gorgeous. Delectable.' He had refilled and emptied his glass several times and his words were beginning to slur, but alcohol did not seem to have reduced his desire in the least. He patted his knee. 'Come on over here.'

'I like it where I am.'

'Just one little kiss.'

Jill knew what was likely to follow one little kiss. She shook her head.

'Ah, come on! How can someone looks as hot as you do grudge a man a little while in Heaven? And it wouldn't be all on one side, I can promise you. Did you know that Indians – the ones in Asia, I mean, not the Native Americans – reckon that a woman gets eight times as much pleasure from sex as a man does? That must be really something. You're going to come and come. I'm hot, believe me, and I know how to please a lady.' The forced smile vanished and was replaced by what she could only think of as a leer. His voice was husky. 'Listen, lady, you'd best accept that it's going to happen before we get back to shore. One way or the other. You ever been tied? It's a lot of fun. Plenty rope aboard. Relax and we'll both enjoy. Not lesbian, are you?' He shrugged. 'Nemmind. What is it you say over there? Lie back and think of England.' He began to specify in detail how he would go about giving a lady pleasure. Jill tried not to listen but there was a sickening fascination in his words which demanded attention.

He was talking himself into the mood for

action. When he decided that the time for words was past and leaned forward to get to his feet, Jill decided that the time had come. She feinted to port, tossed the towel over his head and darted along the starboard side-deck. She heard a roar behind her but when she dropped into the shade of the cockpit, grabbed a winch handle out of its pocket and turned, prepared to sell herself very dearly if at all, he was still sitting on the fore hatch.

She waited. Her mouth was dry. She still had her glass in her hand but its contents had spilt. She put it down carefully on one of the seats and folded the towel beside it. She was shaking and her knees seemed to have turned to rubber. When he came after her, she would make it clear that his attentions were unwelcome. She would have no objection to doing him permanent damage but she would try to stop short of killing him. He might have a thin skull. She practised a few underarm swings with the winch handle.

But, although he was uttering a variety of angry noises, he was not coming after her. Had he given up so soon? It seemed unlikely, but perhaps her rejection had got through to him and he was ashamed to face her. Or else the daiquiris had gone to his legs. She took deep breaths and tried to think calmly, to think of words which might calm him, to think of cruel tricks which might emasculate him.

When her hands stopped shaking, she studied the controls. Beside the companionway was a dashboard not wholly unlike that in her car and a key in its place. She turned the key and under her feet the engine began to mutter.

The sound and vibration caused a stir up in the bow. Ed Marsh (she could not bring herself to think of him as Ed nor as Mr Marsh) was shouting again. He seemed to be calling for help. It could be a ruse. Clutching the winch handle, she stepped up out of the cockpit and took a few paces closer. He was twisting uncomfortably to look at her.

'Go down into the cabin,' he called. 'See if you can find a razor. Or a sharp knife. Or some white spirit. Or paint remover. Or something. Don't just stand there with a goofy expression, help me!' The slurring of alcohol had been replaced by the shrillness of desperation and bad temper.

She took another pace towards him while trying to fit a meaning to his words. Then his body language gave her the clue and suddenly it came to her. She remembered the man, Joe, with the varnish brush. Ed Marsh had seated himself on the hatchtop while it was still tacky. The warmth of his body would have hastened the curing of the synthetic resin and he was now stuck fast by his copious body hair. Jill felt light-headed with relief. She wanted to crow with laughter. It couldn't have happened to a better person.

Carrying her winch handle in case he managed to tear himself free, she ducked under the awning again, made a quick visit to the cabin to collect her dress and returned. The cockpit was not encumbered with controls. She pushed what was evidently the gear lever forward and *Laughing Girl* began to ease ahead. There was a single throttle lever in the forward position and she pulled it back. The yacht's stern settled and she gathered way. Jill span the teak-and-metal wheel until the bow settled roughly where she thought they had come from. The roll turned back into pitching, but slower than before. The yacht had a good turn of speed under power but held straight when she released the wheel to put her dress on.

Very slowly, the coastline came closer and more and more detail became visible. Jill paid no attention to the noises coming from the bow. She picked up what she thought were the landmarks which she had noticed on the way out. Soon, she recognized buildings near the mouth of the yacht basin. She took the engine out of gear and went below. Ed Marsh's trousers had been thrown carelessly on to a bunk. It took only a second to find his car keys. But taking his car would be a criminal offence. She helped herself to some dollars for cab fare. There was a wardrobe between the main and fore cabins, but a quick inspection revealed that Mr Benjamin was not in the habit of leaving clothes aboard. Good! She restored the keys, rolled the clothes up and took them into the cockpit.

The yacht picked up speed again. The bow wave gurgled. *Laughing Girl* was laughing.

Jill was sure of the landmarks now. She lined the yacht up with the mouth of the yacht basin and eased the throttle half-closed. Relief was flooding through her. There were too many witnesses now.

Ed Marsh had lowered his voice. He was pleading now, but her heart remained hard. The dock came closer. There were people carrying gear to a large motor-cruiser and the crew of a schooner were hoisting sail. Jill pulled the gear lever into neutral. *Laughing Girl* slowed, lost all way and nuzzled gently against the timbers as if glad to be home. Jill restored the winch handle to its place and stepped ashore, carrying the bundle of clothes. As she did so, she gave the hull a push with her foot. *Laughing Girl* began to drift. Ed Marsh let out a howl.

Jill walked to the office. When she looked back, people were gathering at the end of the dock and she could hear laughter. She was tempted to let matters take their course, but the boat was Mr Benjamin's pride and joy. The same man was still in the office doorway, keeping a watchful eye on the comings and goings.

'Mr Marsh is adrift on *Laughing Girl*,' she said. 'You'd better go and rescue him. No hurry.'

She threw the clothes into the dock and went to find a cab.

Eleven

Jill was back in the hotel by the early afternoon. Her favourite under-manager was on duty. As he handed Jill a new key-card for her room, he recognized her mood of anger and upset and offered to escort her to her room. This, Jill knew, would have led to another friendly flirtation. Even if she had not been rather off men for the moment, it was not an exchange which she would have welcomed. She declined politely and made it clear that any visitors asking for her were to be identified but not allowed near her room unless on her clear and personal say-so. She collected her computer and files from the safe and headed for her room in order to start trawling through the emails which had undoubtedly started building up again.

In the impersonal but usually friendly cocoon of her room, there were signs that her few possessions had been disturbed. The maid would have had no call to open the drawers. It would, she supposed, have been easy enough for somebody to bribe one of the housekeeping staff to open the door. She could have asked for a change of room, but what would be the point? Nothing had been taken. By custom, she was supposed to feel violated, but the attention was not unexpected and she had forestalled it. Even so, the world was becoming an increasingly hostile environment. If she brooded on it, she would reduce herself to a nervous wreck.

For once, there was no colleague waiting to take her to dinner. She was hungry. She phoned room service. Oltech could afford it. Then she locked her door, put a chair under the handle and settled down at her leisure to catch up with her researches. Late that night, she went to bed well satisfied. A pattern was emerging – not distinct enough yet to make out all the more important faces, but a pattern nonetheless.

Sunday was going to be a waste of valuable time. Americans, even those outside the Bible Belt, took the day off and she had gone as far as she could with her researches until she could consult. She decided to go along with Mr Benjamin's plan for her. A conducted tour of the Everglades along with a crowd of other tourists should be safe – about as safe as it could get and far safer than kicking her heels between the hotel and the Bayview shopping centre with Ed Marsh and God alone knew who else lurking on the streets. Her casual sundress had a pocket. Rather than carry a handbag which could have been easily snatched, she put a few dollars and a handkerchief into a small purse and she was ready.

The hired car which picked her up was luxurious. Transport by limousine was becoming the norm to Jill; her own magic vehicle was going to seem utilitarian when she got back to it. She was driven by a coloured chauffeur who was polite and competent but answered her few questions simply and precisely and remained otherwise silent. They left Interstate 75 and soon were on smaller roads. The countryside was very flat, broken by occasional stands of what the driver told her were Melalucha trees, an introduced species.

Mr Benjamin, or his agent, must have outlined a program to her driver. They turned into an area landscaped with specimen trees. As instructed, Jill browsed among other tourists in the gift and souvenir shop and bought a ticket for a ride on a tractor-drawn train of small carriages which took her past flamingo pools and through gardens rich with botanic specimens from worldwide.

Her driver was finishing the remains of a sandwich and a Coke on a seat in the shade. 'Better get some lunch, ma'am,' he said. 'Ain't much of a lunch where we go next.'

Jill bought a barbecued chicken leg and a fresh orange juice at the snack bar and ate it under a different tree – the driver seemed to prefer not to share a tree with his passenger. Still feeling rather empty but uncertain of the meaning of the other snacks on the menu, she returned to the car and was wafted onward. They began to see waterways. Ten miles brought them to a reception building fronted by a car park bustling with coaches, cars and parties of visitors being marshalled by guides.

Her attention was caught by the many crowlike birds with iridescent plumage. The driver said that they were grackles.

'And the other ones?'

'They're grackles too. Female ones.'

The female grackle was smaller and plainer than the male. Jill decided that they were sexist swine and went in to buy her ticket for the airboat tour. It was proving to be a busy Sunday. There were coachloads ahead of her and she was allotted to the tour which would be the last of the day.

It was easy to pass the waiting time. There was sunshine and shade, grackles to watch and the coming and going of the airboats.

There were anglers in dinghies, though she never saw any of them catch a fish. She met a couple from St Louis who wanted to know all about Scotland. An airboat skipper on standby took her under his wing and explained that the Everglades might look like a prairie but that most of it was a shallow river, fifty miles wide, hidden beneath sawgrass and reeds but with open waterways and lagoons. He became quite lyrical about the wildlife, much of it to be found nowhere else, and he bemoaned the loss of ninety per cent of the wading bird species. The original inhabitants, he said, had been Seminole Indians and their descendants still lived nearby – Muskogee-speakers near what he called Alligator Alley and the Hichiti-speakers in small villages along the Tamiami Trail.

The crowd had thinned out by the time that her trip was called. The last thirty or so passengers were packed into a craft with an overhead awning. The skipper helped Jill to a seat at the very front beside a very fat woman who insisted on telling amusing anecdotes about her not very amusing children and grandchildren. Two large motors started up and the aerial propellers drove them forward. There were no hills. The limestone ridges, known as hammocks, were rarely more than three feet high, but they carried jungly strands of mahogany, strangler figs and what her mentor had called gumbo-limbo. She saw dwarf cypresses draped with Spanish moss.

Their mode of progress was not the quietest. As they made their way through meandering canals and lagoons or skated over narrow beds of reeds or lilies, the skipper had to stop his motors and drift from time to time, to make himself heard as he pointed out the comical anhingas on low branches, hanging their wings to dry after fishing, or the short-eared head of a marsh rabbit as he rose on his hind legs to survey his territory. He showed them an alligator but, to Jill at the time, it seemed to be a disappointingly small one.

When the vessel made a sudden turn into a bed of reeds or sawgrass, the passengers assumed that the skipper was taking a short cut just as the boat was designed to do. But in a sudden silence the skipper explained grimly that one engine had cut out. The boat lacked a reverse gear and in any case could only be steered by balancing the two engines, so they were good and stuck. He tinkered with the engine for a few minutes, tried the starter several times, then gave up and used a mobile phone to summon help.

It was the beginning of an hour of boredom. Mosquitoes were making an appearance but the skipper had a can of insect-repellent spray and was liberal with it. He helped the time to pass by telling them more about the wildlife, the history of the Everglades and the original inhabitants.

At last, when he was beginning to run out of interesting facts, a similar airboat came to assist, but the reeds cushioned its approach and, lacking precise steering or a grip on the water, it failed to penetrate them and come alongside. There was more cellphone traffic. They waited again. Their skipper explained that, because airboats do not have a reverse gear, if the other vessel had managed to force itself alongside it might have become just as firmly stuck.

A smaller boat, with a single fan and a rudder, arrived and began to transfer passengers to the other large airboat, four or five at a time. Jill, being at the front of the airboat, was among the last five passengers to await transfer. The other four clambered cautiously into the smaller vessel.

'That's enough,' said one of the men. The smaller boat pushed off.

'Hold on,' Jill cried.

'Don't worry. I'll be back.'

Jill felt a momentary twinge of suspicion, but one of the passengers being transferred had been the fat woman – Americans, she had noticed, tended to be either very fat or else skinny keep-fit enthusiasts. She waited. The small boat returned but, as she was preparing to cross, the big airboat with all her former fellow-passengers started up and roared off.

Jill shouted after it, but her voice was drowned by the drone of the two engines and their propellers. She was left with the two skippers. 'Stay cool,' said one. 'That craft's tight-packed. We'll give you the rest of the guided tour.'

Left with no sensible alternative, Jill climbed across and the smaller boat skated off, leaving the original airboat in the reeds and awaiting the attention of an engineer. The two men made no attempt to point out the sights to her even when a pair of birds which she thought were ospreys could be seen building their bulky nest in a dead tree.

At first, they seemed to be following in the way taken by the larger boat. Jill soon lost her sense of direction when their course seemed to be indirect and by waterways which showed little signs of traffic. She had lost sight of the ripples left by the larger boat. The sun was getting low in the sky and it was not where her recollection of the outward journey suggested that it should be. Surreptitiously she studied the two men. They resembled each other, being flat-faced and hook-nosed and with bronzed skin. She thought that they were avoiding making eye-contact with her.

They emerged at last into a lagoon, larger than any that she had seen so far. In the middle, the man in control throttled down and coasted to a halt. 'Here?' he asked.

Jill waited, expecting to be shown an alligator or a water moccasin.

'This is good,' said the other. He drew out the gear lever. 'You reckon?'

'No marks, the man told us. And she can't swim.'

Jill's heart leaped into her throat and remained there, beating frantically. In quick succession she read several different meanings into the exchange but she did not like any of them.

'Seems a waste,' said one of the men. 'We could have some good fun first.'

'Ain't no way. Any trace of that and they'd know it wasn't no accident.' He looked at Jill for the first time. 'Too bad, girl, but somebody wants you out of the way – I don't know who.'

They came at her together. She fought but the most that she could manage was to scratch one man's face in a desperate attempt to leave some evidence behind. A child of our time, she knew about DNA. The boat, flat-bottomed though it was, rocked wildly but the two men had no difficulty keeping their balance. Jill was picked up and tossed unceremoniously over the side. She broke the undulating, glassy surface with a great splash.

Jill's suspicions had already been halfway aroused and the brief exchange of words had given her a few seconds to prepare. Even if she had been forewarned and wholly alert she could not have fought off the two men, but at least she had time to draw several quick, deep breaths, to store extra oxygen in her blood. The water, when she hit it, was surprisingly warm – swimming outdoors, she was accustomed to water which had descended from the mountains. Part of her mind must have been anticipating danger because she found that, beneath her fear, her mind was racing along, driven by the need to survive. Without surfacing, she turned on her back and, adopting a froglike stroke, began to swim towards where she thought that she had seen the nearest trees. Above her, the surface was still broken by the ripples from her entry, enough, she hoped, to hide her underwater movement.

One of her hands found a ball of detached water-weed and she clutched it. She was beginning to run short of oxygen. If she went further, when she surfaced eventually she would betray herself by gasping for breath. She had only made the length of a tennis court, but it would have to do. She let herself drift very slowly towards the surface, pulling the ball of water-weed over her face, and forced herself to lie still, maintaining her position with small underwater movements of her hands and breathing deeply but as slowly as she could manage. The water-weed tried once to float away and she made a small splash as she retrieved it, but the noise must have been taken for a rising fish. She anchored the weed more firmly by use of her teeth. It tasted foul and hampered her breathing, but the weed hid her face and the rest of her was under water.

The men's voices were muffled by the water and unintelligible, but she forced herself to wait patiently. An age went by. When the men were silent, she was afraid to breathe and then afraid not to in case her breathing was more audible when she started again. Perhaps the sunset noises of the wild were giving her some cover. The temptation to start swimming again was almost overpowering but she knew that it would be the wrong tactic and she fought it down. At last she was rewarded by the sound of the boat's motor starting up and she could breathe freely. The sound diminished with distance. When she allowed herself to surface, spitting out the weed, there was a faint mutter in the distance but the only traces of the boat were some lingering ripples still rolling across the water.

Jill turned and swam for the only visible trees, a long way off. She kicked off her shoes. Her thin skirt clung to her legs but it was not hampering her movements and she was damned if she was going to be rescued semi-nude. If she was going to be rescued ... The light was fading fast. Something brushed her leg. Too smooth for an alligator. A fish? Please God, not a water moccasin!

Her friend had mentioned Alligator Alley. Where was it and was she swimming towards it? Alligators, he had said, were especially aggressive during the spring breeding season. This was spring. They grew up to fourteen feet long – more than two and a half times as long as herself. She tried to swim without splashing. She could have managed a fast crawl but that would surely attract any underwater predators. There were crocodiles here too. She stuck to a compromise between breast stroke and a dog-paddle and slid through the water with a minimum of disturbance.

There was little more than a trace of daylight when she neared what seemed to be a shore. But was it a bed of reeds? Or, worse, sawgrass? She swam parallel to the shore, hoping for inspiration.

There was a gap in the growth and something that looked very much like muddy ground among the tangle of undergrowth. Trying not to think of leeches she struggled to the shore, kicking away weed. The water tried to drag her back, her feet slid in mud, but she managed to crawl ashore. She was told later that the gap had almost certainly been the landing place frequented by an alligator, but happily the possibility never occurred to her. She was on land, that was what counted. Foliage brushed her face.

She looked around and listened. There were no lights but she thought that she could hear the distant rumble of traffic from further inland. Perhaps she could walk to civilization, but if she was on an island she might have to swim again. She started to feel and stumble away from the water, but the tangle was thick. She could hear things moving and almost immediately she put her face into what was probably the web of the golden orb weaver, a huge but harmless female spider whose webs are both spectacular and strong. She freed herself as best she could and retreated to the waterside. The little plot of mud had begun to feel like home compared to the unknown around her. She had had enough. She wanted to sit, but all kinds of creatures might be crawling around her feet. There could be coral snakes, she knew, and two species of rattlesnake. There were poisonous plants – poison ivy, poisonwood and machineel. Her mentor the off-duty airboat skipper had been articulate about the dangers. She would stand still and wait for rescue or daylight. Even standing still in darkness presented difficulties. She had never realized how much she depended on the faculty of sight for her sense of balance. She found a tree-trunk that she could lean against, and damn the spiders! A bobcat howled, not very far away.

She had no watch with her and no idea of the passage of time except by the wheeling of such stars as she could see. She only knew that she was cold and swaying on her feet with tiredness but still too scared to sit down when she was jerked awake by a sound like a footfall on the mud. It could be an alligator. In desperation, she shouted and heard a large bird take off and flap ponderously away across the water.

The next sound to penetrate her exhaustion was the soft mutter of a small outboard. She dragged her eyes open and saw that a light was approaching over the water. The moon had come up, veiled by thin cloud, and she could make out the shape of a small dinghy with a man in the stern.

She waved. She shouted. She screamed.

She was sure that he would go by without seeing her. But suddenly a brighter light flicked on and a beam played over her and went out. The dinghy turned and puttered towards her. Some yards out, it halted and the motor stopped.

'You stranded?' a deep voice called.

'That's right.'

'Can you come out to me? Damned if I want weed around the prop again. I got out of my usual channel and I was clearing it for the tenth time when I dropped my knife in. After that I had to clear the weed with my fingers. That's why I'm out so late. Been fishing. Got some bass and a couple of brim.'

While he spoke with gradually diminishing volume, Jill had waded and swum out, braving the alligators and water moccasins. Aided by a hand under her arm, she heaved herself over the stern, knocking her elbow on the hot outboard. Her dress had almost dried on her but now it was soaked again and she was feeling the night-time chill. She groped her way to the middle thwart and sat down. After her tree, it was luxury.

While she waited the night away she had been thinking many thoughts, but out of the confusion had arrived one decision. 'Take me to the police,' she said. 'Or the sheriff or whatever.'

Twelve

The hotel staff seemed unperturbed by the return of a guest in the middle of the night, muddied, mosquito-bitten, shoeless and dishevelled, deposited from a car with flashing lights on the roof. Jill padded barefoot across the hallway, collected her computer from the safe and persuaded the night porter to escort her to her room. She had managed to hold herself together through her ordeal, through the long boat-ride with the garrulous angler and through a lengthy interview with the sheriff's department, but she felt her resolve slipping. If she did not share the burden she would collapse under it.

Her room seemed undisturbed. Her mobile phone was still in the drawer. When it was in her hand, she paused. One person who knew her plans for the weekend had been Mr Benjamin himself. A moment's thought assured her that there could have been no point in inviting her to investigate and then resorting to hired assassins when she began to glimpse the truth. He was the boss. If he had wished the truth to remain submerged, he need only have told her to drop it. Even more convincingly, she had become convinced that he was a person who could be trusted, the one stable figure in the turbulent world of oil. She needed desperately to unload her mind. Perhaps if she dumped all her new-found knowledge on somebody else, nobody would any longer have a motive to kill her.

With shaking fingers she keyed in the only number to come into her head. Despite the hour, Mr Benjamin responded immediately. At the sound of Jill's voice, he asked sharply, 'What's wrong?'

Her sense of relief was out of proportion. 'Things have been happening. I've a lot to tell you.'

'Urgent?'

'Very, I think.'

'Not on the phone and from a hotel room, if that's where you are.' There was a pause while he considered. 'I'll come for you.'

'Where are you?'

'Back in Miami.' (Jill felt the advancing dangers take another step back. She had imagined him still in California.) 'I'll give a few rings on your mobile when I'm getting close.'

She was suddenly aware of her state. Her

dress had dried on her for a second time but she doubted if it would ever be wearable again. 'Can you give me twenty minutes?' she asked.

'Easily.'

Jill caught sight of herself in the mirror. He hair looked like that osprey's nest. She was tempted to call him again and ask for an hour, but she was rushing towards comfort and safety. Instead, she hustled herself in and out of a shower, washing her hair as she went, wrapped her hair in a hand-towel and hurriedly dressed in presentable clothes. She was brushing her hair under the hair-drier provided by a helpful management when her phone double-beeped four times and cut off. The mirror assured her that her hair looked only a little more weird than some of the styles that she had seen on models on the catwalk. With a little luck, Mr Benjamin might take it for the very latest fashion. She might even start a trend. She gathered up her computer and disks and descended to the lobby.

Mr Benjamin was already at the door in a shining black Bentley, complete with left-hand drive. He dismounted – there was no other word for it – and opened the right-hand door for her. The doors closed with gentle purpose and she thought again that even her new 4 x4 would feel a little shoddy when she got back to it – she could say *when* rather than *if*, now that she was with Mr Benjamin. The Bentley oozed down the ramp and moved off between tall buildings still bright with lights.

'Now, don't say anything about company business until we're out of the car. It hasn't been swept for a while and it would be an obvious place to bug. We can talk about something else. What was behind the message that reached me about strange doings on my boat?'

Jill might have thought his obsession about electronic bugs paranoid, but in the light of recent events she was ready to go along with any conspiracy theory and it now seemed no more than common sense. At the time, the virtual kidnapping and subsequent implicit threats of Ed Marsh had been menacing and had somehow undermined her sense of security but now, in Mr Benjamin's company, they looked lightweight and almost frivolous. The only reputation to suffer would be that of the absent Mr Marsh, so Jill spoke up clearly for the benefit of any possible listening devices and began on the story. The funny side of it had been dimmed by the ominous overtones, but in his relaxing company she found that she was consciously building up towards the climax.

As she spoke, she watched Mr Benjamin's expression as passing lights played over it. From the moment when she revealed that there had been no other company aboard *Laughing Girl*, his face developed a frown which grew blacker as the story progressed. Then, when Jill reached the point at which Ed Marsh had found that he was stuck fast to the varnished fore-hatch by the plentiful hair on his backside, he began to laugh. 'No more while I'm driving,' he said. 'This could get dangerous.' He continued to chuckle gently but Jill noticed that his driving remained impeccable.

They had left the city by the almost empty freeway. Jill thought that they were not far from the yacht basin where *Laughing Girl* was berthed. The ground showed up as landscaped rather than open country. They stopped at a gate in a wall topped by metal fencing. A security camera stared at them dispassionately, a voice quacked at them, Mr Benjamin activated a remote-control device on the dashboard and the gate slid open.

The ground rose gradually in front of them to a height of about twenty metres. 'Highest mountain in southern Florida,' he said. 'Entirely artificial, but it gives us a view and cuts down the danger from a storm surge.'

In the light of the headlamps and the subdued street lighting, Jill judged that there were about a dozen spreading houses, well separated and screened by carefully arranged trees. A security guard, walking with two dogs on leashes, saluted the car. They turned into a driveway. The house was modern and yet the choice of materials and the complexity of gables was reminiscent of something older. A trellis with climbing plants in full flower sheltered the main door but a wide garage door was sliding up and the Bentley nosed inside to park beside a 4 x 4 which could almost have accommodated Jill's car in the back. Lights came on, apparently of their own accord, and the big door settled down again with no more than a faint hum and a click.

He led her through an internal door and a short passage into a large living room, deeply carpeted, comfortably furnished and masculine in style. In switching on subdued lighting he must have touched another control because curtains drew themselves closed across the window wall. Air-conditioning had established the room at a comfortable temperature, and the outdoor humidity was noticeably absent.

The armchairs around a big stone fireplace were large and deep but he brought forward a smaller, more upright chair from by a side-table, saying, 'You'd be lost in one of those monsters. I only keep them for the benefit of some of my enormous friends. You'll be more comfortable in this. And now, I think you need a drink.'

He removed her computer to a glass-topped coffee-table and brought her what she identified as a brandy and soda. 'Relax,' he said. 'You look as tensed up as a harp. You've had a shock but it's over now. Are you hungry?'

Jill had not eaten since the chicken leg which she had taken at lunchtime, some-where in the Everglades. 'At the hotel,' she said, 'I didn't think that I'd ever eat again. But I've just realized that I'm starving.'

Mr Benjamin nodded, left the room for a minute and returned. 'There will be something to eat shortly,' he said. He took a seat by her side in one of the large chairs. 'When you're ready, and not before, take up your tale.'

Jill took a sip of her brandy. A smoothness suggested that it was very good brandy. She cleared her throat. It seemed most expedient to start by finishing the tale of her adventures with *Laughing Girl*. When she came to the denouement, he straightened his face. 'I shall have to have a very serious word with Ed,' he said. 'My instructions to him were perfectly clear and he had no business making serious passes at my guest. But I'll leave it for a day or two until the humour of his situation has left me. Otherwise I might crack up in the middle of reading him a lecture, which would surely do away with its impact. I'm sorry that you were treated to an unpleasant experience. All the same, I wish that I could have seen it. I'm told that my fore-hatch now seems to be finished in suede.'

Jill tried to smile but her face seemed frozen. Delayed shock seemed to be catching up with her and facts were fitting themselves together with uncomfortable clarity. 'It didn't seem funny at the time and, frankly, it looks worse in retrospect. If you let me tell you the rest of the story, you'll see why. I'm only just beginning to see how it adds up.'

He looked at her over the rim of his glass. 'One moment.'

A manservant who, from his face, might have been Mexican or Puerto Rican, came in with a tray. Jill noticed that he was smart in a white jacket. Did nobody go to bed in this house? He placed a small table in front of her and laid out cutlery, wine glasses and an omelette with mushrooms, bacon, onions and herbs. At a nod from Mr Benjamin he withdrew, still in silence. Jill had finished her brandy. Mr Benjamin produced wine and poured two glasses.

'Go ahead.'

Jill thought that he probably meant her to go ahead with the rest of her story, but she preferred to interpret his words as meaning to eat. She put her fears and distress to one side and ate with tears of pleasure in her eyes. There was cheese in the omelette as well, and the wine was very good. When she had finished, she brought her mind back, forced her voice to remain steady and tried to tell her tale as if it had happened to a third party. She described the events leading up to her immersion in the Everglades. When she spoke of her vigil in darkness, surrounded by the noises of the night and not knowing if the first boat to come by might not bring back her would-be killers, the fears which she had stoutly held at bay swept over her again. Her voice broke at last and she felt the tears coming. 'I'm sorry,' she said shakily. 'I don't mean to give way to the vapours, but it's all been a bit much.'

He reached out to her and she took his hand. It felt warm and dry and comforting. 'You've done very well,' he said. 'I was just thinking that you'd held yourself together better than any girl I know would have done ... and better than most of the men, what's more.'

That assurance was the last straw. She lost

her voice completely. Tears overflowed and she had come without a handkerchief.

'This is damned uncomfortable,' he said suddenly. He got to his feet and pulled her up. She thought that she was about to be kissed. She decided that a kiss would be welcome and that she would respond with enthusiasm, but instead he led her to the deep couch and sat down with her. 'Now I can hold your hand without feeling that my arm's being broken.' He produced a spotlessly clean handkerchief from his pocket.

'When you're ready again,' he said, 'I have to know what you told the sheriff. You did make a report to the sheriff?'

She blew her nose, wiped her eyes, took some more of the brandy and cleared her throat. 'I had to. I realized that my driver would certainly notice that his passenger had never returned; and the men would have to report my absence as an accidental drowning in case my body turned up. I'd had time to think about what you'd probably want me to say. Or not to say. So I told the sheriff that the two men had tried to rape me and I'd jumped overboard and swum underwater to the bank. The deputies seemed to know who the men were. I suppose I'll have to go and identify them?'

'Possibly. Yes, that was well thought out.' He paused. 'You've told me the exact words that they said?'

'You saw the implication, then?' Jill choked, recovered and went on. 'It means that your cousin was going to kill me. He was the only person who had reason to believe that I couldn't swim. That's why he was prepared to get rough with me, knowing that I wouldn't be able to tell you about it. He was going to come ashore with a story about my falling overboard. When he didn't manage to ... to do it, they put together another plan to drown me. I'm sorry, really I am. Your cousin...' she finished in a wail.

He let go of her hand and instead put his arm around her shoulders. 'It came as a shock,' he said, 'but Ed was never my favourite cousin. If it wasn't for the business connection I'd probably never see him. His business is failing. A large heap of dirty dollars or a promise of a lucrative contract from one of our rivals would buy him. I will deal with young Ed later,' he said grimly. 'At a guess, he spread some of that money around and masterminded the second attempt on you. If we can prove anything, the law can have him. Otherwise, I will personally see to it that he is very, very sorry.'

'How?' Jill asked curiously. She would rather have relished thinking of Ed Marsh in some highly distressing situation.

'I don't know how yet,' Mr Benjamin said,

to her disappointment. 'Rest assured that I am more than capable of finding a way. Meanwhile, I can only apologize on behalf of the family and congratulate you on having managed so very well. You've been very brave.'

Jill felt far from brave and to be reassured in such a confident manner was too much. Her composure drained away and she buried her face in the handkerchief. Mr Benjamin comforted her with a hug and, after a respectful pause, began to kiss the tears away. He comforted her in other ways. She was in great need of comfort and she was truly comforted.

Jill's two previous ventures into the realm of Eros had left her with the impression that sex was a mildly pleasant pastime but far from what it was cracked up to be. She had wondered, in fact, what all the fuss was about. However, on waking in a strange bed in a luxurious bedroom, to a bright day and birdsong, she realized that her previous lovers had been selfish and callow youths. Mr Benjamin had not only proved to be a man of vigour and sophistication; she had been surprised to detect during their raptures that he was concentrating more on giving than on taking pleasure. She had been lifted to what she had previously thought to be the slightly disappointing summit of pleasure and then carried onward and upward to a plateau of delight which she had believed to be an invention of romantic novelists and then kept there for longer than she would have believed possible.

Her languorous musings were interrupted. She was brought down to earth by the arrival of the impassive manservant with a breakfast tray. Her attempt to pull the sheets over herself were frustrated by the fact that she was lying on them, so she remained still and tried to pretend that she was a figment of his prurient imagination. He seemed to go along with the fiction.

She was drinking excellent coffee and nibbling at the unfamiliar array of foods which the Americans choose for breakfast when Mr Benjamin came in. He looked fresh and ready for the day, lacking only the jacket and tie. He pulled up a chair and sat down.

'My dear,' he said earnestly, 'I would have preferred to spend time assuring you that last night represented a high point in my life and that I will remain eternally privileged for what passed between us. My only worry is that you might feel that I took advantage of your innocence and your distress.'

Jill felt that the speech called for a gracious reply in similarly rolling periods, but an assurance that she had thoroughly enjoyed the experience seemed out of keeping with maidenly modesty so she just smiled and shook her head.

'Good. Unfortunately, we are rather short of time, so I will ask you to take it as read. We will certainly return to the subject on some other occasion. Is that acceptable?'

Jill nodded.

'Thank you. I feel that we should get you away from here as soon as possible, so a car will be calling for you before very long to take you to the airport, and if the police lay their hands on your attackers you can come back to testify. Unfortunately, there's no way that we can conceal the fact that you survived yesterday's attack. It's a pity that you had to involve the sheriff but, as you said, the two culprits must have been known to the organizers of the boat trips, so they would also have been bound to notify somebody in authority that their passenger had met with an unfortunate accident.'

'The deputies said that they had had a phone call which cut off.'

'That would figure. So, following your complaint, the sheriff will now be looking for the two culprits. The failure of the attempt will get back to the instigator.'

'The sheriff may not get very far,' Jill said. 'The deputies seemed very concerned because the fisherman who rescued me was part Seminole and he seemed to think that where he found me was just inside an Indian reservation. I didn't realize at the time, but the men who dunked me in the water looked at least part Indian.'

'They probably would be. There are few if any pure Seminole left but thousands of mixed blood – anybody with one-sixteenth or more Indian blood qualifies for the benefits. Yes, that could certainly hold things up,' Mr Benjamin said. 'No police force, not even Federal, can go on to Indian land without the permission of the tribal council. And now, you'd better get dressed. I want you on that plane and I must prepare for this afternoon's meeting. I'll come over soon to bring you up to date and take action.'

'Yes, but listen,' Jill said urgently. 'I haven't really told you the important bits yet. On Saturday – was it only the day before yesterday? – I had most of the afternoon and all evening to fill in, and I was jittery and nervous. I was afraid to go out on my own in case your cousin was lurking and I think I'd have gone mad if I'd had to sit still and twiddle my thumbs, so I set about co-ordinating in my computer all that I'd found out. I made some phone calls to Scotland and picked up some emails which had been waiting for me.' She broke off. 'Where *is* my computer? It's got everything—'

'Keep your cool. I'll fetch it. You start getting dressed.'

He left the room. Jill put aside the tray and got out of bed. Her bare toes sank into the thick carpet. She seemed to recall that most of her clothes had been left in the living room and she had no intention of prowling nude through a strange house which might be filled with Latino menservants, but as soon as she began to look for some garment to cover her nakedness she found her clothes, neatly folded on a chair. They seemed to have been laundered and ironed during the interim but she had no time to think about that. She had only just begun to get dressed when Mr Benjamin returned with her computer and the small box of disks, placed them on a dressing-table and pulled up a chair for her.

'Show me,' he said.

Jill felt more naked than naked. 'Let me get dressed first.'

'This is more urgent. Anyway, you're a pleasure to the eye.'

Jill was doubtful but nevertheless flattered. She forgot to be self-conscious while her interest was caught in booting up her computer and calling up the appropriate material. 'Here we are,' she said. 'I transferred everything on to a single disk, arranged person by person. There may be some people that I've missed, outside consultants and contractors and so on, but in the main I think it's fairly complete. Would you prefer that I didn't tell you anything about where the financial information came from?'

He shook his head. 'We're long past that point. And this house is secure.'

'Well then. There may be some secret accounts that Geoff Dubois didn't manage to find, but I doubt it. Most people came up clean. Some of those who received transfers from other accounts are quite innocent. You can ignore this chap.' She moved the cursor to the name of George Wallis. 'I rather wanted him to be caught out, but it seems that he'd bought a flat for his lady-friend to occupy and sold it again when she ran off with somebody else.'

Mr Benjamin was looking at her with his eyebrows up. 'How on earth do you know all this?' he enquired.

'The transaction didn't look secretive enough to fool the world. Only enough to hide it from his parents or some other girl-friend. So I phoned a friend with an address close to his. She knew about it from what she called the babe-vine. Moving on, I had my suspicions of this fellow –' she halted the cursor at the name of Mr Syme, the depot manager – 'and it turns out that he's been

247

banking a whole lot of money, but it's in irregular amounts and, anyway, some things I've heard suggest that he isn't part of the main conspiracy but that he's been on the fiddle for himself, hiring out your equipment while it's lying idle. When we had that meeting about the strike, did you notice that there was a reaction when I mentioned hiring and leasing? I'd guess that the men knew about it and got a cut to turn a blind eye, but we'll never prove that. I suggest an unexpected stocktaking, instead of taking stock on a date fixed months ahead.'

'That's a job for you, as soon as you get back to Scotland. And you could take an interest in disciplinary procedures against the shop steward. You may be safer if the staff see that you're preoccupied with side-issues.'

Jill moved the cursor onward. 'This is probably one of the principal culprits. You'll note that he made a visit to Caber Beta at the right time. Geoff only got on to him because he used a credit card for any real extravagances and settled the credit card accounts by direct debit from a very secret account in Holland where several large deposits had been made. After that, Geoff tried to check where those deposits had come from, but he met a dead end.'

She continued in the same vein. After a

minute or two, Mr Benjamin was looking grim. 'You've moved mountains,' he said. 'I never hoped for half such a result.'

'Are you going to confront them?'

'Not on the basis of what you've got so far. That information was illegally obtained. I'll have to think hard about our next line of action. Is that the lot?'

'Not quite. I got my hands on a copy of the geological survey map that everybody's been studying. But I also got Geoff to pull me a copy of the original digital survey out of the company server. I compared the two of them, the night before last, and they don't even fit where they touch. I'm not much of a geologist, but I think the report you were shown was doctored to give a very pessimistic picture. As I read it, there are much bigger oil reserves and much cheaper to extract.'

Mr Benjamin usually showed the world a face registering calm assurance but Jill could see that this news was causing him to think furiously. 'Now you've given me the key to the whole riddle,' he said at last. 'I think that I shall have to succumb to a dose of twenty-four-hour flu.'

'Really?'

'Not really. A pretext to put off the meeting for a day and summon one or two members of staff to come and discuss company operations with me at my sick-bed. I shall have some dispositions to make. And now,' he looked at his watch, 'your car is due.'

Jill jumped up and hurried to put on her bra. She was conscious of a momentary disappointment. She had hoped to do some serious shopping in America, where clothes were definitely good value. But he was right. Florida was not the place for her.

Thirteen

Jill landed in Scotland late on the Monday. Fine spring weather was shedding an evening glow over the earth but after Florida she felt the cold as crisp, clear and invigorating. Her parents admired her new tan but when they asked about her trip she gave them a highly censored version. Her car was waiting for her at home, dusty but otherwise unsullied and with no more miles on the clock than were accounted for by the return from Dyce Airport. She rewarded her father with a gift from the duty-free shop. The car, as she had expected, felt small and utilitarian at first but soon the honeymoon feeling was restored.

She gave herself the Tuesday off and slept away her jet-lag and her reaction to her adventures. When she returned to the office on Wednesday, the building was throbbing with rumours, few of which bore more than a passing resemblance to the facts. Ed Marsh's embarrassing attachment to *Laughing Girl* had been funny enough to deserve a

251

mention in a Florida paper but there had only been passing mention of an unidentified female companion and so had made only a brief side-bar in the popular British tabloids. Jill's complaint to the sheriff, however, had been relayed to the British media along with her name. Any story with a mention of rape is grist to that particular mill. According to Sheila Dobson, the original and fictitious version was being diverted further from the truth with a wealth of imaginary and salacious detail. Reporters were calling regularly for an interview or a quote. When the first reporters caught up with her, Jill thought of claiming the privileged privacy of the violated but instead played down the story as grossly exaggerated. With that they had to be satisfied for the moment. An eventual trial would bring the juicier facts out into daylight. Her mother showed all the signs of imminent nervous breakdown but was eventually satisfied by an assurance that her wee lamb was quite unhurt. In the end, Mrs Allbright managed to convince herself that her daughter had not been raped or otherwise molested and her concern lapsed.

From an office computer she accessed her email. Of the fourteen messages awaiting her attention, eleven were from David Banion. She printed them out for later study in the privacy of home.

The curiosity of the staff had already been whetted by the police enquiries into the attack in the office car park. Jill was aware of being followed by the curious eyes of her colleagues. She was also aware of other eyes following her around, of a car reappearing in her mirror or the same inconspicuous person in her peripheral vision. Her anxieties flooded back and she was ready to jump at shadows. She thought of phoning the police, but when she mentioned this to Mr Benjamin in the course of one of her daily reports, she could hear amusement in his voice over the phone. 'Don't let it fret you,' he said. 'Check him out if you like. He should be from Grant and Wallace. They're supposed to be the best in the business. They've supplied us with bodyguards in the past when staff have been threatened by cranks or kidnappers and we've never lost anybody yet.' This gave her a warmly enclosed feeling but she felt illogically guilty at having given rise to such expense and she was of too independent a spirit to welcome uninvited mothering.

She was soon certain that the most usual of her shadows for the latter part of the day was a heavily silhouetted man in a green Vauxhall Cavalier. When she left the office that evening and spotted the car parked in a shaded corner of the office car park, she bypassed her own car and walked over to rap on his closed window.

The man had a square face topped by tight brown curls. His only distinguishing features were his prominent eyebrow ridges and unusually alert eyes. Looking downward on his seated figure, she could see that he was very deep-chested. He pretended at first that Jill was not there and then, when that ploy was obviously not going to work, he lowered a window. 'Can I help you?' he asked.

'I hope that you never have to,' Jill said. (The man blinked. Her words registered with him.) 'For my peace of mind, tell me who engaged you.'

He took a moment to think. Blank denial must have seemed inappropriate, because he said, 'That would go against client confidentiality.'

'Then I'm going to call the police and report that I'm being stalked.'

He sighed. 'I only know that the instruction came from the USA. Miami, I think.'

'And you work for?'

He sighed again. 'Grant and Wallace.'

'Fine. But I'm sure that any danger is long past by now,' Jill said, 'so you may as well knock off and save the client some money.'

'We're contracted until the end of the month.'

'In that case...' Jill had never been one for looking gift horses in mouths. 'You have a mobile? Give me the number. I'll summon you if I need to be rescued. Or if I want something heavy lifted.'

He grinned, bringing to his bland face an unexpected charm. 'Give me your mobile,' he said, 'and I'll key the number in for you.'

While he was inputting the number, she asked, 'What's your name?'

'Pentecost.'

'If I do have to call you, don't take five days to arrive.'

Jill made her statement to the police about the attack in the car park and made a tentative identification of the two men from among a set of photographs. She was reprimanded for absenting herself, but not very severely. It seemed that the total disappearance of those men and the weight of a major oil company had combined to mitigate her offence.

She was in regular touch with Mr Benjamin by mobile phone but he was uninformative – understandably so, she thought. He gave her full authority to act in the matter of the depot, so she set about arranging for the surprise stocktaking.

Mr Fiddich muttered to himself when she demanded his assistance and he muttered even more when she insisted on his being present throughout the process, which was carried out by a small team representing several departments and overseen by a man from the outside auditors. He muttered some more when, after some very expensive equipment was found to be missing, he was firmly instructed that the depot manager was to be dismissed and prosecuted. A field engineer of proven honesty was called back to take over the running of the depot. It was left to Jill to track down the missing equipment and recover it from the firms which, innocently or not, had it on hire.

'The idiot was being ripped off,' she told Mr Benjamin. 'If I was going to get into fraud, which I'm not, at least I'd grab my fair share. The plant-hire firm may have driven a thief's bargain but it does seem to have taken on the deals in fairly good faith. They have forty-two of our thirty-one-foot non-magnetic drill collars and some stabilizers.'

'That represents money,' he said.

'It does. But it will leave their customers in a serious hole if we insist on the return of the goods now, and I've checked with our engineers – we won't need them for six months, maybe more. We may need a return favour in the future. So I've negotiated a fresh deal – if you agree.'

She had telephoned the plant-hire firm, concealing her identity and asking for quotations for the hire of the same equipment, so she had a fair idea as to what the going rates might be. When she quoted figures, Mr Benjamin's chuckle came clearly over the air. 'Go ahead. But six months may be the limit.'

Mr Fiddich's indignation hit a new high when Jill, after obtaining a briefing from the Personnel Director, told him that he must also deal with Herb Spicer, at present bailed on the drugs charge. He drew himself up and glared at Jill across his desk. 'He is a member of my staff,' he said, 'and it is my decision how I handle the matter.'

'Of course it is,' Jill said amicably. 'But he has been dealing drugs on company premises. Miami will be observing how you cope with it.'

'As reported by you?'

'Of course.'

'I may as well tell you,' Mr Fiddich said with a rare show of real spirit, 'that I resent being told how to manage my own staff by...'

Jill's amicability vanished. 'Go on,' she said grimly.

Mr Fiddich had been on the point of

hinting that Jill had ensnared Mr Benjamin. But he could only guess at a relationship. It was dawning on him that Jill had overcome her earlier uncertainties and that if she had indeed become the mistress of one of the company's supreme panjandrums he might be very unwise to quarrel with her. 'By somebody who is ... clearly very much under the influence of Miami.'

'What were you really going to say?' Jill asked. Her voice was cold enough to send a shiver up his back.

Mr Fiddich shook his head. There was a pause. 'I forget,' he said at last. 'Anyway, the man hasn't been convicted of anything.'

'He doesn't have to be convicted. You can dismiss him if you are satisfied that he has misbehaved.'

'There are procedures.'

'Follow them.'

'He could sue us if he's acquitted.'

'He's made some very damaging admissions. But if you really think he may get off,' Jill said, 'you can always suspend him.'

'I suppose I could – on full pay.'

'Yes. Of course, if he does get sent down in the end, all that pay to a drug dealer – one of your own staff, as you pointed out – in return for no work, may not look good.'

The General Manager rubbed his face. 'Suspension without pay might look worse if he does get acquitted.' He paused. 'Will you sit in with me?' It was a capitulation.

The meeting took place next day, in the presence of the Personnel Director and with a secretary to take notes. The union had provided a lawyer from a local firm, but so truculent was Spicer's manner that the lawyer was reduced to arguing procedural points and legal technicalities. Spicer, now that Jill set eyes on him for the first time, turned out to be a lean man with a thin moustache and watery eyes.

Mr Fiddich had begun the meeting in a manner which was almost apologetic but, as Spicer became more defiant, the General Manager developed an unaccustomed firmness. 'There can be no question of allowing you back to work until the court case has concluded. You have admitted dealing in drugs on the company's premises.'

'I was tricked into it,' Spicer said sullenly. This was palpably untrue but several minutes were wasted while the union's solicitor tried to make bricks without straw.

'Be that as it may,' Mr Fiddich said at last, 'you have been charged with the offence. To have you back, working on the same premises, would set an appalling example to other employees and send the wrong messages to the police and to the business community.'

Spicer shook off the lawyer's restraining hand, jumped to his feet and leaned across the desk. 'Ye fozie, spreckelt, gruggled auld bogger,' he ground out. 'Fuck the business community and fuck you too. This is a jist acose o ma union activities. Well, ye'll nae win aff wi't.' After a few more seconds of rant, he rounded on Jill. 'And you, ye ill-gien wee limmer. There's mair nor me as wad wheep the hide aff yer erse. Ye'll catch it, ma quine. If een disna get ye anither wull. Seestu, yer heid's up for grabs.'

Jim Gordon and the lawyer had hold of him by now or Spicer, who was dribbling with frustrated fury, would have clutched at Jill's throat. They pulled him back to his chair. Charles Fiddich, properly incensed by such behaviour and none too pleased at being addressed as a 'flabby, spotty, wrinkled old bugger', spoke up. 'You're fired,' he said distinctly. 'Mr Gordon, call Security.'

The lawyer could only shrug and follow as his client was led away by two security men, still raging. The atmosphere in Mr Fiddich's room took seconds to resume its usual placidity.

'I get blamed for everything,' Jill said with an attempt at lightness, but her mouth was dry and her voice was not quite steady.

The Personnel Director looked at her shrewdly. 'Don't refine too much on it,' he

260

said. 'Threats are easy to utter, but the people who make them usually have more to lose than to gain by carrying them out.'

'All the same,' Jill said, 'I wish I could be sure that I knew who he meant.' She used her mobile phone to warn Mr Pentecost to be wary. She might need him after all.

It was more than three weeks after Jill's return from Florida before Mr Benjamin managed another visit. Jill quite understood. She knew from the ripples which had washed up in the Aberdeen office that there were events in train which were better not put on paper or discussed over the phone. In the meantime, she continued her life while keeping a wary eye out. Among senior staff members, in particular Mr Fiddich and Mr Pringle the Finance Director, she met hostility and covert obstruction, although without an overt threat. She was, however, becoming popular in some quarters. Younger male members of staff had recovered sufficiently from their initial awe to try chatting her up and she received several invitations. David Banion was offshore for most of the period, so she accepted one or two of those invitations, but drawing the evening firmly to a close between a final drink or snack and your-place-or-mine. Who she was saving herself for was not quite clear in her mind.

Suddenly, the media were full of rumours which circulated the office as hard fact. Oltech was said to have been successful in its tenders for the lion's share of the new exploration sections. Omulco had lost out. Jill kept her eyes open. All the faces around her seemed to be wearing happy smiles but several of the smiles might have been forced.

Two days later, Mr Benjamin arrived on his promised visit, bringing Jill's computer back to her. The weather had reverted to dull and drizzly and his plane was late. Jill, in her new car, collected him from Dyce in mid-afternoon. He expressed admiration for the car though she could see that, privately, he considered it more suitable for the use of his housemen. They visited the office and he gave his approval, almost absently, to some proposed changes to the management structure which had emerged from the senior staff meetings. He promised a full statement to staff as soon as the tenders received governmental approval.

Immediate business finished, he suggested dinner and the two walked down together to Jill's car. In the car, he said, 'It's too early for dinner. That was only an excuse to get you out of there. Drive to somewhere where we can talk freely.'

Obediently, Jill drove out through Torry and up to Nigg. She parked on the cliffs near the coastguard station. The view over the North Sea was totally obscured by mist and low cloud.

'You've come to tell me the punchline,' Jill prompted.

He chuckled. The warm sound was becoming comfortably familiar to Jill. 'On condition that you tell me what it was that you held over the head of your friend the protester.'

'No. I promised. Anyway, I can make a good guess at what happened, because what I'd have done in your shoes fits pretty well with what I've seen going on here, give or take a bit.'

'What would you have done, in my shoes?'

'You don't mind talking in the car? It hasn't been checked for bugs.'

'Not really. The past is history now and those affected must have a good idea of the story-line. Just have a care on the subject of where our information came from. Well? What would you have done?'

Jill gathered her thoughts. Mr Benjamin put up a hand and stroked the back of her neck and then laid his arm gently across her shoulders. She supposed that she had given him the right. She found that his probable actions had laid themselves out neatly in her mind. She said, 'I would have let the formal meeting go ahead and approve tender figures based on the false geological survey. But, at the same time, I would have had a small and trusted team preparing tenders based on the real survey, and those are the tenders that I would have lodged.

'I know that the company was successful in bidding for several sections. True?'

'Subject to confirmation, yes.'

'And I hear that Omulco lost out badly. So I would guess that the man who was the contact with Bill Boddam was acting for Omulco.'

'He was. We've confirmed that much.'

'By making use of the slush fund which isn't supposed to exist?' She felt his arm jerk. 'You don't have to answer that.

'I suggested to you that Mr McRobb and Mr Pringle were almost certainly in the conspiracy. They would have been taking bribes but that sort of greed doesn't stop at the first and easiest pickings. They'd know, or think they knew, how the shares were going to move. I think they'd also want to make a killing in shares. Not just buying Omulco shares, but selling Oltech. Do they call it "selling short"?'

'They do. Selling shares that you don't have, in the expectation of being able to buy them at a lower price before you have to deliver them. That's where you can make the biggest profits but as easily lose a whole lot more money than you've really got.'

'Well, that's what they did,' said Jill, 'because when the news came out and Oltech shares shot up and Omulco went down, they and several others were walking around with smiles on their faces, but those smiles looked about as natural as camels in a church.'

'I can't say that I'm surprised,' Mr Benjamin said. 'We've been watching the situation as it developed and our best guess is that they're in hock, miles away over their heads. Broke and likely to stay broke for a long, long time.'

Jill decided that Mr Benjamin's 'best guess' resulted from an illegal monitoring of bank accounts and share movements by Geoff Dubois, but there was to be no mention of that source while there was any possibility that the conversation might ever be monitored. The fact that the principal, almost the only, evidence had been illegally obtained would preclude prosecutions, but it seemed that a poetic justice had been meted out after all. 'And serve them right,' she said. 'But there's one more person who's been looking like a hen trying to lay a brick.'

'Charles Fiddich?' Mr Benjamin suggested.

'Yes.' Jill looked at him in surprise. There had been no unexpected transactions in any bank account traceable to the General Manager.

'A little more research brought it to light after you left for home. Somebody had purchased a nice little property in the Caribbean in his name.' He pronounced Caribbean in the American way, with the accent on the second syllable. 'Shall we walk a little? Or would you be too cold? There's a breeze getting up.'

So the time had come for exchanges which were definitely not to be overheard. 'I shan't be too cold,' Jill said, smiling. 'Thanks to the generosity of your bonus, I have a tweed coat with a Goretex lining.' She picked the coat off the back seat and, quitting the car, shrugged into it.

He joined her as she locked the car. His knee-length coat was of soft glove-leather and he had a hat to match. They set off gently along the road. 'Touching on the matter of bonus,' he said, 'I have another cheque for you. Not so much a bonus as compensation for the danger and discomfort you found yourself in. To be brutally honest with you, it's for rather more than I proposed at first, but my father was adamant and I couldn't disagree. Your efforts have averted a major financial disaster and opened the door to long-term profitability and steady employment for all your more loyal colleagues. I tell you this now so that you won't think that it is in any way contingent on the other topics we still have to discuss.'

A van came up the hill, crawling carefully through the gathering mist. Jill drew well off the road to let it by. The precaution reminded her of something. 'Herbert Spicer, the man who first brought me into all this by calling the strike, was raving mad when we suspended him. He was shouting that more than one other person was after my blood.'

'I wouldn't worry too much about it,' Mr Benjamin said, in a comforting echo of Jim Gordon's opinion. 'There's no profit in revenge. We now have a list of everybody who sold Oltech shares short. Each of them is already in severe financial trouble. Company employees among them will be advised that their prospects with the company are not good and they will all be warned that, if any harm comes to you, their names and Mr Spicer's threats will be drawn to the attention of the police. However, you must have noticed that you have been under discreet guard?'

'I noticed. I was scared out of my wits until I realized that they were on our side. He's about fifty yards behind us now.'

'We'll keep them on until we can be even more certain that all threats to you are in the past.'

'I'm very grateful,' Jill said.

'Don't be. We owe it to you. To continue, Mr Fiddich will be allowed to retain his property in the Caribbean but he's in too deep a financial bind to have any hope of keeping it.

'He will be leaving the company very shortly. The man that we had in mind as his successor is being brought back to take over. His will be a six-year contract. Would you care to be his depute for that period? You have exactly the local knowledge that he will lack.'

Jill was staggered. Her mind was zig-zagging around the longer-term implications of what he had said when he spoke again.

'Before you make up your mind, I have an alternative proposition for you.' He turned and pulled her towards him. 'My principal reason for coming over was to ask you to marry me. I think I could make you happy and I know that you could do the same for me. We get along just great. You're clever and you're beautiful. You have strength of mind. And life never gets dull while you're around. I don't need an answer straight away, but give me a hint.'

The leather against her face felt soft and yet very masculine. Jill thought that he might be the perfect husband. He was cultured. He was rich. He was very good to be with. She felt safe with him. But the pampered routine of a Miami wife would not be for her. She would not fit into the Miami office – the vernacular and the way of life were too strange to her; and yet, the idle life would drive her to distraction. How empty could a life get if filled only with pleasure? Jill pulled back and looked at the mist. The countryside was hidden for the moment, but it was her countryside. It had hills and valleys. It had sunshine and rain. Endless sunshine could become as boring as eternal flatness.

'You're a very dear friend,' she said at last. 'And I'm very tempted. But I could never settle in the Florida climate and you certainly wouldn't want to move over here. Sex with you was out of this world and I'll be bitterly hurt if we don't repeat the experience every time you come over here.' David Banion, she thought, would forgive her. Or he need never know. 'But not marriage. Certainly not just yet. Can you forgive me?'

He tightened his clasp again. 'I'll forgive you,' he said slowly, 'on one condition. If you'll tell me the hold that you have over that young man Boddam, the protester. Just between ourselves.'

Jill felt that she could hardly refuse him anything. 'Between ourselves? You promise?'

'I promise.'

'*Really* promise? Not to go and tell everybody else, in confidence?'

She felt him shake with laughter. 'I honest-to-God promise,' he said. 'I might tell my father. It's been driving me mad but it stops right there.'

'All right,' she said. She looked over her shoulder but Mr Pentecost's broad figure was half hidden in the mist and well beyond earshot. 'If you break your word I'll never sleep with you again.' They turned and began to walk back towards the car, arm in arm. Mr Pentecost seemed to have vanished. 'When we were teenagers, his father was the minister of a village church and they lived in a huge old manse. His girlfriend was my very best friend – I won't even tell you her name, we'll just call her Mary. She lived almost next door to the manse. They had a big fight one time and while she was still furious with him she told me the whole story.

'Whenever his parents were away, he used to smuggle her into the manse and they'd go up to his room and fool around. I don't know if they were doing it at that time, they were both quite young, but there was certainly some heavy petting going on. If his parents had found out, there would have been hell to pay.'

'I bet,' Mr Benjamin said softly.

'Yes. His father was a minister of the old school, believing that sex had been invented by the devil for luring the young into his power. The manse was a great Victorian barrack of a place with no central heating and his room was about a mile and a half from the nearest bathroom. To save him doing the trip in the middle of a freezing night, Bill kept a gallon can with a screw-top beside his bed. It had held motor oil, once upon a time.

'One afternoon, they were together on his bed and he wanted a pee, so he rolled over and took up the can. And just as he was starting to pee, she turned after him and put her tongue in his ear.'

Mr Benjamin could see where the story was going. 'Oh my God! No!' he said.

'But yes.' Jill voice was beginning to quiver. 'Suddenly he got big and he was good and stuck. I wouldn't know much about it, but I'm told that the blood can get in but it can't get out.'

'That seems to be the way of it.'

'So they were in a real pickle. If they called an ambulance, the story would be all over the village and it would get back to his father who, as I said, was a minister of the old, strict school. They didn't have a car, he wasn't going to get on a bus with a large can stuck to his front; and even if they took a taxi he wouldn't have dared walk into Casualty that way.'

Mr Benjamin gave a shout of laughter, muffled by the mist.

'You can probably imagine this better than I can,' Jill said. 'Anyway, Mary went for her brother, under a vow of absolute secrecy, and when he'd had his laugh he decided to help. His first idea was to take a hacksaw to the neck of the can but Bill absolutely vetoed that idea.'

'I can imagine. So how did it all end?'

'As you'd expect, in anticlimax. They took a file and very gently filed away at the metal. That worked in the end. But Mary said that Bill couldn't spend a penny for weeks afterwards without crying. Well, you can imagine how little he'd enjoy having that story spread around. I threatened to go on a chat show and tell it.'

'You couldn't tell that story on a chat show!' Mr Benjamin sounded shocked.

'Anything goes on British chat shows these days. And now,' Jill said, 'let's leave the sordid subject. Would you be more interested in dinner or in a visit to your hotel room?'

Mr Benjamin kissed her with a foretaste of passion. 'Those are both good ideas,' he said. 'I'm glad you thought of them.'

They returned to the car. Jill drove through the dying daylight, following the intricacies of the one-way system to his hotel. They dallied in the bar until a table was ready for them and then ate with gusto and a comfortable expectation of the pleasures to come.

They had reached the stage for coffee when Mr Benjamin's mobile phone sounded. With a word of apology, he took it out. He listened for a minute, made an acknowledgement and disconnected. 'I'm sorry, my dear,' he said. 'It seems that dalliance will have to wait for a little longer. That was Jim Gordon. We have a serious problem. I think we should both return to the office.'

Fourteen

Jill's car was only a stone's throw from the back door of the hotel. The drizzle was continuous at the worst level, just enough to necessitate the windscreen wipers but not enough to wash the traffic spray and diesel smear off the screen. She had to feel around before she recalled how to work the washers. Oncoming lights reflected off the street surface. As she drove, she said, 'Don't tell me until we get there. In these conditions, I need all my concentration.'

'Right. And I need time to think.'

She had become attuned to his body language and, as she drove, she could feel the tension emanating from him. The office car park was empty except for Jim Gordon's hatchback and the very old Ford Prefect sometimes borrowed by Fay. There were lights on in the tall block – her friends the cleaners were at work. They went in by the side door and took the lift.

In the lift, he said, 'Two men went missing from Caber Alpha. Bad enough in itself, Jill, but it comes at the worst possible time. Your Department of Trade and Industry has been putting off making an announcement about the allocation of the new sections because of the smear campaign against the company over safety and pollution. This just might make them decide against us. It could be disastrous for the UK company and none too good for the parent one.'

The lift stopped at the ninth floor. The drone of vacuum cleaners met them. Jim Gordon must have seen the car arrive, because he was waiting at the lift with files under his arm. He limited his greeting to a single, unintelligible syllable. He looked harassed. 'May we use your room?' he asked Jill. 'Mine's rather small and the cleaners have already been through your floor.'

'Of course.'

In the lift again, the Personnel Director said, 'I called one of the telephonists to come in and man the PABX.'

'Good idea,' Mr Benjamin said.

In her own room, Jill wheeled the executive desk chair round to the end of the desk so as to be one of a trio rather than the figure beyond the desk. They seated themselves.

'The first I knew about it,' Jim Gordon said, 'was when a *Press and Journal* reporter phoned me at home, wanting a quote. They usually call me first if it's anything to do with people. I came straight in and phoned the rig and found that it was true. Two men were booked aboard from the first helicopter this morning and they clocked on for some minor maintenance work, but now there's no sign of them. Presumably they're lost – nobody's sure yet how or even when. I can't reach Mr Fiddich and,' he looked at Jill reproachfully, 'your mobile wasn't answering.'

'I switched it off to save the battery,' Jill said. In Mr Benjamin's company, she had not expected to need it.

'The press was quick off the mark,' Mr Benjamin said bitterly. 'And I suppose that everybody from the Scottish Executive to the Health and Safety Executive and from Brussels to Westminster will have been lobbied by tomorrow morning.'

Jill was immediately overcome by an awful certainty. The incident was a propaganda exercise aimed at nullifying Oltech's bids. But would anyone, even for the money involved, sacrifice two innocent lives? She recalled her swim in the Everglades. Yes, they undoubtedly would. But the thought of two lives snuffed out for gain almost overwhelmed her. They had been the lives of men who had attacked her, but somehow that had almost been an introduction. Had those acquaintances left widows? Children? She reached for the files that Jim Gordon had laid on the desk. 'Are these their personnel records? May I look?'

Mr Benjamin spoke to the switchboard. Any calls from the media were to be met with a flat statement that no comment could be made until the deaths were confirmed and more facts were known. Any other callers were to be put through to Miss Allbright's room. He put down the receiver and went on to ask a series of questions, some of which Jim Gordon was hard put to answer. What rescue attempts had been made? Had the police been informed? The coastguard? The Health and Safety Executive? How had the press found out so quickly? What was the phone number of the rig? He wanted to speak to the OIM.

In reaching for the phone again, he looked in Jill's direction and checked himself. 'What are you grinning about?'

'Don't be too hasty,' Jill said. Relief was settling over her. 'It's a put-up job. Look.' Clipped to the inside of the file-cover of each was a photograph, a duplicate print of the original taken for the man's identity badge. 'These are the two men who came after me in the car park.'

'You're sure?'

'Positive. I saw them at close range – only

for a second or two, but long enough for photographic images to be fixed in my brain. James and Angus Fraser, it says here. Same address for each of them. Brothers, at a guess. It would be a hell of a coincidence if just those two were involved in the attempt on me and then they were lost overside in an accident at just this time.'

There were a few seconds of silence so deep that they could hear a cleaning machine operating several floors below. Mr Gordon gave a startled grunt.

'What are you suggesting?' Mr Benjamin asked. 'That the two had outlived their usefulness and were dropped overboard? Or that the deaths were faked?'

The concept was too fresh to have been digested. 'I don't know,' Jill said. 'Either. You said yourself that if you're prepared to throw enough money around you can arrange anything. Well, the people who've been trying to prevent the company's bids succeeding have big, big money at stake and they must be desperate by now. This could be a last throw of the dice. Either way, dead or vamoosed, if I'm right and we can show it, this company gets off the hook. Could two men be smuggled ashore from a rig?'

'If they ever went offshore in the first place,' Mr Benjamin said. He too had been thinking furiously. 'The easiest fiddle would be to bribe somebody to fake the records and then report that they were nowhere to be found.' He knuckled his forehead, thinking furiously, but Jill could see that he had already begun to relax. 'We must let everyone know of the connection,' he said. 'First the OIM. Then the police.'

'You speak to the OIM,' Jim Gordon said. 'Here's the number. No doubt somebody will tell me what this is all about in due course.'

Jill slipped out of the room, taking with her the two photographs from the files. She took to the stairs. On the tenth-floor landing, she met Fay. 'I was on the way down to look for you,' Jill said. 'I didn't expect to find you up here.'

'We all moved up one after you left us,' Fay explained. 'There's a new wifie taken over the general office and the typing pool.' She would have gone on to explain the new dispositions at some length, but Jill was in a hurry.

'Can you get the others together? I want to know if anybody knows these two. Or knows somebody who might know them. They're the two men who tried to mug me in the car park and now they're supposed to have got lost off a rig but we think there's something fishy about it.'

Fay handed back the photographs. 'If they

two are in it, there'll sure as hell be some-thing fishy.'

'You know them?'

'My man does, just to nod to in the pub, because they're friendly with Herbie Spicer. Remember him?'

'I remember him,' Jill said. 'Do I ever!'

'My man pointed them out once. They're the Fraser brothers. After that, I kept hearing things. They're bad lots. If they're drowned, good riddance I say.'

'So do I,' Jill said. 'But they may have faked it, just to get the company in trouble. Their names and faces will be in the *P and J* tomorrow and I see that they live in one of those busy tenements in King Street, so they surely can't be hiding out at home – somebody there would be sure to phone the papers about dead men come to life. Have you any idea where they might be hiding out?'

Fay shook her tight yellow curls. 'I wouldn't want to know the likes of them. I'll ask the other girls. And I'll phone my man. You'll be in your new room? Leave those photies with me.'

Jill hurried back upstairs and resumed her seat. Mr Benjamin was on the phone – to the police, Jim Gordon whispered. 'We con-tend that there are three possibilities,' Mr Benjamin was saying. 'One, that they're already out of the country; but it would have had to be set up in a hurry, so that seems unlikely. Two, they're hiding out somewhere. Or, three, that they have been deliberately knocked off, with the same end in view.' He listened to a voice from the receiver. 'All right, Superintendent. Four. They may have met with a genuine accident but, frankly, I do not believe it. The two men who tried to take Miss Allbright's computer off her turn out to be offshore employees of the same company and are reported missing from a platform just when the adverse publicity could do that company most damage. In my book, that is just too much coincidence to be for real. You agree? Well, whether you agree or not, I hope that you'll keep looking for them alive and on shore and let the media know it when they approach you for quotes.'

He finished the call and sat back. 'I could tell from his voice that he thinks we're clutching at straws. But those two won't have got abroad yet. If this was a long-planned move, they'd have timed it for before the bids were in. As you said, Miss Allbright, this is a last-ditch attempt to reverse the final decision. I guess I'd better report to Miami,' he said.

In company, Jill noticed, she was Miss Allbright again. Fair enough. 'What did the

OIM say?' she asked.

'He could only tell me that the men were recorded as arriving on the platform and then it was later reported to him that they couldn't be found. He says that a thorough search was carried out by men that he can trust. He's going to start an enquiry with the two men who'd have to be bribed if the arrival of those men was to be faked but I did find out that it was one of those men who reported them missing. I guess that's about all we can do from here just now. I'd better let my father know what's going on.'

'You could hold off for a minute or two,' Jill said. 'I've set my scouts to work and...' There was a knock at the door. 'This may be the scout-mistress now.'

She opened the door to Fay. The formidable cleaning lady appeared quite timid in the company of such seniority. Even her prominent bust seemed to have developed a subservient droop. She refused a chair and preferred to stand.

'What have you found out?' Jill asked.

'Well now,' Fay began. 'I phoned my man and he phoned another man, Doug Phillips – you widna ken him, but he gaes fishing wi the Frasers. He says they hae a bothy on the coast, awa beyond Stonehaven. They keep a lobster boat moored there.'

'A bothy?' Mr Benjamin enquired.

'Fisherman's hut,' Jill said. 'Can you tell us exactly where this bothy is?' she asked.

'My man's away to see Doug Phillips and hae him mark it on a road map and he'll leave the map with yon telephone lassie doon the stair.'

Mr Benjamin got to his feet and shook Fay's hand. 'Well done, Mrs...?'

'Ferrier.'

'Well done, Mrs Ferrier. Would you be insulted...?' He produced his wallet. Fay shook her head. A note passed between them and he escorted her to the door. Fay's blonde curls were held high again.

'Which is all very well,' Mr Benjamin said, resuming his seat, 'but it presents us with the next problem, which is how to handle the matter.'

'The police must be told,' Jim Gordon said stiffly.

'Of course. And then what?' Mr Benjamin, deep in thought, was looking at the ceiling but he stabbed a finger in Jill's direction as he made each point. 'We sit back and let matters take their course? What course do they take? That superintendent sounded totally unconvinced. It's late evening. The few men he has available will be busy with late drunks and early prowlers. So the most we could expect would be one car with two officers – unarmed, I guess, in this country, and one of them possibly female – driving up as close as they can get and knocking politely on a door where, we hope, two, maybe three, very tough guys are in hiding with strong motivation not to be found. So either we have two dead cops to get blamed for or, if those men get enough warning from all the strobe lights, they find the place deserted and we never can prove that we didn't lose two men off the rig.'

'The place could be deserted anyway,' Jill said. 'They may genuinely have gone out to the rig and then been brought back by their fishing boat. In which case, they could have been landed anywhere. They may even have landed on the Norwegian side. Or, if they were heading back to their bothy by fishing boat, they might even not have got back there yet.'

Mr Benjamin was nodding. 'If the police are called out and find the place empty, they'll stop paying any attention to what we tell them. I think I'd better go and take a look, before they have time to go further afield. You two stay here and man the phones—'

'You are definitely not going alone,' Jill said.

Mr Benjamin looked at her, uncertain whether to be annoyed by her presumption or pleased by her concern. 'I'm only going to observe – from a distance if possible.'

'Four eyes are better than two. And somebody should observe the observer, just in case.'

Mr Benjamin had known Jill for long enough to know that once her mind was made up it would take a bulldozer to shift it. 'Very well,' he said. 'You drive. Gordon, you man the phones.'

Jill was far from sure of the wisdom of their expedition, but she had no intention of showing herself up as a timid female nor of provoking Mr Benjamin into an outpouring of male, porcine chauvinism. Any such clash, she was sure, would bring to an end a relationship which she hoped to find both rewarding and physically satisfying. She cut through to Anderson Drive, left Aberdeen by the Bridge of Dee and bombed along the dual carriageway in the general direction of Dundee. She had had no earlier excuse to try out the paces of her new car. She found that it could exceed the speed limit by a margin which would surely attract any prowling traffic car on to their tail, in which event she had every intention of explaining the urgency of their errand. The outcome, if they played their cards right, should be the planned covert visit but with police backup.

No traffic car was so obliging as to intercept them and Mr Benjamin seemed quite unperturbed by their speed. By the light of a carefully shielded pencil-torch, he deciphered the map which had been left for them. Of course, she thought, he was the sort of man who would certainly have a torch in his inside pocket. They passed Stonehaven and turned off on to the old coast road, sometimes almost on the cliff edge and sometimes deviating further inland. There had been ample traffic on the main road, enough to turn driving her new car in the wet conditions from a thrill into a battle with the dazzle of oncoming lights, but once they had turned on to the coast road they had the world, apart from a few scattered villages, to themselves. Where, she wondered, was Mr Pentecost now?

The rain soon stopped. A streak of moonglow in the parting clouds was reflected in the texture of the North Sea.

'About another mile,' Mr Benjamin said.

There was a layby ahead. 'I think we should keep Mr Gordon posted,' Jill said.

'Yes. All right.'

She drew into the layby. Mr Benjamin had already produced his mobile phone and keyed in the Oltech number. He spoke briefly with the switchboard operator and then with Jim Gordon. When he ended the call, his voice sounded tired. 'So far, six newspapers, two radio stations, a TV network and two members of Parliament, all wanting confirmation and, in the case of the media, quotes.'

'We'd better have guessed right,' Jill said. 'Please God!'

The stress was evident in his voice and Jill sought for a way to relieve it. She put her hands on the wheel but she waited before driving off. 'Suppose that they're not there,' she said. 'Suppose that there really was an accident or that they were given a push off the rig.'

'I'd much rather not suppose anything of the sort.'

'Just suppose it anyway. We could light the stove in the bothy, put freshly dirtied dishes on the table, use the chemical toilet if that's what they use, and show the place to the police and the media.'

'Not the toilet,' said Mr Benjamin. 'DNA,' he explained. 'Let's go and find out how much of a problem we have before we start solving it.' He sounded amused, which she thought was a step in the right direction.

The moon emerged through a break in the clouds. Jill was able to reduce her lights to dipped beam, then to sidelights and then, as they neared their objective, extinguish them altogether. According to the map, there was a watercourse which passed under the road and followed a deep cleft down to the sea. The place was unmistakable even by moonlight, because trees had managed to root themselves in the shelter of the gully close to the road, visible in the bare landscape from a long way off.

A rough track, barely passable by car, followed the gully downhill towards the bothy. Where the track left the road, there was a triangle of rough ground outside the field boundaries, dotted with gorse bushes, and Jill drove cautiously off the road. At Mr Benjamin's suggestion, she eased forward to where they could see down the track as well as the inadequate moonlight would allow.

'No lights are showing,' Jill said.

'The shack's probably round a corner and out of our sight. Anyway, they'd be mad to let lights show if they could be seen from the road. I'd better go and take a look.'

'We could wait until they come up,' Jill suggested.

'What happened to that logical brain of yours? One, they have a boat. Two, if they do come up, we're not going to fight them and if they go away we've probably lost them. Three, they could intend to sit tight for weeks, until the fuss dies down.'

'All right. I'll come with you.'

Mr Benjamin sat in the near-darkness

while he considered. 'Better not,' he said at last. 'Lock yourself into the car and watch the track. If you see a series of blinks from my torch, phone the police. You have your cellphone?'

'Yes,' Jill said. 'In my hand. But ... You won't do anything mad? I don't want to have to explain to your father.'

'I'll be careful. I'm a devout coward.'

'I don't belive you. Can't you walk along and look down from the top of the cliff?'

The moon vanished behind thick cloud again. 'That answers your question,' he said. 'I'd probably walk off the cliff. Is your interior light switched off?'

'Yes.'

'Good. The fewer lights we flash around, the better.'

He left the car, closing the door gently behind him. The breeze which was scudding the clouds overhead whirled briefly in the car. She pulled up the button of the driver's door, locking all the doors, and nursed her mobile phone. Her night vision was coming. She could just make out his dark figure as he picked his way cautiously to the head of the track. Moments later she saw a cautious blink of his torch and then he was gone.

The first minute of waiting seemed an eternity. It was silent and it was dark. She thought that she could understand the torture of sensory deprivation. Two cars went by on the road and she closed her eyes to preserve her vision. When their sound had died away, she opened her eyes again but even the faint light which had penetrated her eyelids had set back her night vision and all was black. With nothing to focus on, she wondered whether her eyes were focused at all. Was she, in fact, looking down the track? Would she see the tiny flicker of his torch?

She made up her mind to be patient. He would not be so foolish as to use his torch. He would be feeling his way with his feet, going carefully to move in silence. This could take time.

After more minutes, anxiety overcame her reservations. She put aside the mobile phone and opened the car door. She might see better if she groped her way to the head of the track.

The man must have been crouched beside the car, waiting. As she came upright, she was seized from behind. She let out one startled squeak before there was a hand over her mouth. His other arm was around her waist and arms and he seemed very strong. A voice in her ear said, 'Another sound like that and I'll break your neck.' The hand, which smelled of fish and tobacco and other things, had turned her head to the very limit and she knew that he could dislocate her neck with a single wrench. Her breathing was also obstructed. She thought that he might kill her without meaning to. If she vomited, perhaps he would take his hand away; but nothing would come.

The cloud cover was broken now and the moon found another rift. Silver light flooded down and by its light she saw Herb Spicer's approach from the nearest clump of gorse. He had to stand on tiptoe to glare into her eyes. 'I telled you,' he whispered. 'I telled you your heid was up for grabs. You're for it now, quinie. You're *for* it.'

'It's the back of the queue for you, Sonny Jim,' said her captor. 'She tried to run me down, so the first grab's mine.' Jill was in no doubt that he was getting pleasure from the clasp of her body. She tried not to think of what might be in store.

Some signal must have been flashed along the road, because a large car, unlit, came ghosting along the road and pulled in behind Jill's car. Even by moonlight, the figure which emerged she could easily recognize as that of Mr Fiddich. He looked at Jill's captor. 'Angus can cope on his own?' he asked.

'With a middle-aged Yankee businessman? No bother,' said the man holding her, who had to be James Fraser, the other brother.

The General Manager of Oltech UK exchanged a nod with Spicer. Either the scene in his office had been a charade or the prospect of money had smoothed over their difference.

Mr Fiddich came closer to Jill. Herb Spicer moved aside to make room for him. 'You little fool,' the General Manager said exultantly. 'I've had your room bugged since the second day you joined the company. And now you've handed me the answer to my problems on a plate.' He paused and tutted. 'No, not on a plate, on a silver salver. I was on the verge of ruin, but now, on top of the loss of two men from a rig, one of the company bosses disappears along with the young tart he took into the firm and promoted over the heads of much better qualified staff.'

The rift in the clouds blew by. Darkness returned. Mr Fiddich's voice came out of the darkness, piling weight on to Jill's despair. 'What will they make of your disappearances, when you're both anchored to the bottom of the cold North Sea? Suicide or running away from disgrace? Who cares? Around tomorrow midday, I'll find that Oltech's accounts have been cleaned out to the tune of millions, traceable to Mr Benjamin. After the stink we can arrange to have made in the media, Oltech won't have a hope in—'

His voice cut off suddenly. 'Boss?' said James Fraser uncertainly in her ear. 'Boss?'

'Whit's agley?' came Herb Spicer's voice. 'Hey...'

James Fraser was turning round, trying to penetrate the darkness, and dragging Jill with him. She was sure that her neck was going to break. But suddenly both grips on her were released. She fell to her knees. When her breath had come back, she crawled forward, away from where she thought danger must be waiting. Her head butted the side of her car. She thought of crawling underneath but there was not quite enough space for her. She might be safe, locked inside. The handle clicked as she opened the door.

'No lights,' said a voice which she seemed to recognize.

She eased herself into the driver's seat and waited. Seconds later, the moon found another thin patch in the cloud. A nightmare figure was rising to its feet. A heavily built man but moving with trained grace. His eyes were black and glaring, like nothing that she could remember. She looked away and saw James Fraser lying prone, his hands behind his back. Herb Spicer seemed to be in much the same state.

The newcomer put up his hands, took

something from his face and stowed it carefully in a pouch. Night-vision glasses, she realized suddenly. It explained how he had managed to follow her car from Stonehaven without showing his lights and why he had waited for the sudden darkness. His voice had sounded familiar and now she recognized him. 'Mr Pentecost?' she said.

'The same. Hop out and open your rear door, please.'

Jill obeyed without understanding. Mr Fiddich was on the ground, just beginning to stir. Mr Pentecost lifted him effortlessly by the slack of his clothing and stuffed him into the back of the car. 'I only had two pairs of thumbcuffs,' he explained. 'If you lock the doors now, that should be enough to hold him. Marvellous what cutting off the blood supply to the brain will do,' he added, 'but the effect doesn't last for long.'

Jill was in a fret to go after Mr Benjamin but she snatched her mobile phone from the car and clipped the hook of the carrying case on to the waistband of her skirt. She pointed her key and locked the doors. 'He won't damage my car, will he?' she asked.

'Not if he wants to walk again.'

'There's another man,' Jill said. 'Benjamin Hochmeinster – your client – went down there. Hadn't we – you – better go down and make sure that he's all right?'

'I don't like to leave you alone with these toughs, cuffed or not. Perhaps I'd better do something nasty to them before I go?'

Somebody, she thought Herb Spicer, whimpered.

Jill looked up at the sky. It was mostly black cloud and there were very few stars to be seen. The idea of being alone with two very hostile toughs and with Mr Fiddich locked in her car, in what seemed almost certain to be total blackness, did not appeal. Every sound would have her jumping out of her skin. That thought was lent emphasis when the faint moonlight faded again.

'I'll go down and find out,' she said. 'You stay on guard here. Here, take my car key. I'll come back for you if we need help. Or I'll phone you.'

'I'm not supposed to let you out of my sight,' Mr Pentecost said.

'You'll be more use keeping these three from interfering or running off.'

Mr Pentecost began a lengthy explanation as to why Jill would be quite safe if she remained in charge of the captives and why he should be the one to go.

Jill circumvented his arguments by walking off in the darkness. The immediate vicinity was clear in her memory and she had her bearings. When the ground dipped slightly and she went from grass on to a hard, rough surface, she knew that she had found the track. She turned left. Mr Pentecost's voice broke off. She should have got his night-vision glasses off him. Perhaps he would use them to follow her up, letting the prisoners flee if they could. She might settle for that.

Dark though the night was, the clouds were not quite as dark as the land and she could make out the silhouette of the skylines of trees and rock walls. Guided by this, by the sense of touch in her feet and by the sound of the water gurgling beside her, she could follow the track, stumbling occasionally. Once, she walked off into the water, but it was shallow; and, when a stumble brought her to her knees for a moment, her hand found a loose, heavy stone. She brought it with her. As a weapon it might prove to be worth its considerable weight in gold. Her shoes were full of water and she squelched as she walked, but the breeze was enough to cover the sound.

After several minutes of this going, the blackness ahead seemed to be opening and she thought that she could see the sea. And hear it. But over the sound of surf breaking on rocks she began to hear the sound of conflict. Something, perhaps the lack of shouting, told her that it was one-to-one.

She broke into a run, tripped and almost

fell, recovered her stone and went on more slowly. Grunts and gasps and shuffling footsteps called her on. Light spread across the ground until she was sure that it was more than moonlight. The track rounded a corner of rock wall and the scene opened.

A clinker-built workboat on a trolley stood on a patch of rough ground which soon gave way to shingle and then to surf. The bothy was roughly built and stood on a rock shelf, out of reach of the highest waves. After the blackness, the light of a Tilley lamp hanging outside the bothy seemed almost dazzling.

Two men were fighting. She had no difficulty recognizing Mr Benjamin although for once his perfect grooming had suffered. The other, Angus Fraser, was the man who had struggled with the passenger's door of her car. Mr Benjamin was clearly the more agile, but Fraser was possessed of a heavy crowbar with which he was launching a series of swings. Any one of these could have taken Mr Benjamin's head off, but the very weight of the weapon made its movement ponderous and gave him time for evasive action. As Jill watched, he ducked under a swing and delivered a punch to the other man's kidney as he slipped past.

Jill came up behind a well-grown holly bush. In her dark office dress she knew that she was too inconspicuous to be noticed by two preoccupied men. There was no doubt that the heavy crowbar was causing Fraser to draw deeply on his reserve of energy and she guessed that Mr Benjamin was waiting for him to exhaust himself.

The graceless dance might have continued until Fraser collapsed but, after a dozen or so swings of the crowbar and evasions by Mr Benjamin, Fraser changed his tactic. He raised the crowbar but instead of the usual swing at the other's head he paused, holding the crowbar aloft one-handed. Mr Benjamin, falling for the bluff, ducked in under the expected swing and instead of delivering a punch to the body received to his own body a blow which carried the force of both strength and desperation. It failed to put him down but he was hurt and backing away, mouth open, winded.

Angus Fraser recognized his chance but his state was little better. He gathered himself for the killer blow but paused for a fatal second to recover his breath, which gave Jill time to rush in.

Something warned Fraser – the sound of her footsteps, a shadow, a change in Mr Benjamin's body language, perhaps all three. He span round and began another swing. Jill was running into it and it was too late to stop. Her only escape from the lethal arc was to let her feet outrun her body, throwing herself flat on her back. The crowbar swung harmlessly above her but she had only postponed the evil moment. Fraser gasped with triumph and swung again. Too late to move, too slow to roll, Jill had one desperate, last fling left. The big stone was somehow still in her hand, half forgotten. She threw it.

She aimed for his head but from her impossible position her aim was awry. The stone whacked against Fraser's hand and he lost his grip on the crowbar. The bar clunked on to the ground. Fraser was nursing his hand but he raised one booted foot for a kick at Jill's head. Jill tried to roll.

Mr Benjamin tackled Fraser from behind, one hand on his throat and the other at his eyes. Fraser gripped his wrists. Mr Benjamin might work out but Fraser was hardened by a lifetime of physical work and, now that they were at close quarters, Jill was in no doubt as to who would come out on top.

The crowbar was almost under her hand. She pushed herself to her knees and grabbed the bar. Its weight surprised her but she swung it with all her might, catching Fraser across the shins.

The fight was over. Fraser howled and began to collapse. Mr Benjamin lowered him gently. Jill, her blood pounding in her ears, raised the crowbar. The world owed her a little vengeance – for her fright in the car park, for the menace of Ed Marsh, for her night in the Everglades. She was ready to split Fraser open or nail him to the ground. But Mr Benjamin caught the crowbar before she could bring it down. 'Enough,' he said. 'Unless you want to get jugged along with the others. He's finished. You've broken both his legs. He isn't going anywhere.'

Instinctively, he straightened his tie and Jill ran her fingers through her hair. She recovered her mobile phone from where it had skidded away along the ground. It seemed undamaged. They left Fraser lying there, still howling, and returned up the track. The clouds were blowing away to the northward and full moonlight was established.

Jill stopped suddenly and they faced each other. 'We'll have to call the police,' Jill said. 'And an ambulance. We can let Mr Gordon attend to all that. But what about the media? The story of the arrests will have more impact if we let them go ahead first and announce the double fatal accident.'

Mr Benjamin tilted the face of his watch to catch the moonlight. 'Most of the morning papers will be in print by now,' he said. 'Let them be wrong about the accidents. Breakfast radio and TV will contradict them. All very satisfactory.'

Near the head of the track, they met four figures on the way down. James Fraser was now linked by his right thumb to Mr Fiddich's right thumb; and Herb Spicer by his left thumb to Mr Fiddich's left. Mr Pentecost was shepherding the three, who stumbled awkwardly. 'I was coming in case you needed backup,' Pentecost said.

'We seem to have managed,' said Mr Benjamin.

Jill keyed the code for the Oltech offices. While she waited for the operator to answer, she stood nose-to-nose with Herb Spicer. 'Wha's heid's up fae grabs noo, ye coorse wee bugger?' she asked.